The Prize

A Novel about Bullies and Victims… and What Drives Them

American Book Classics™
An imprint of American Book Publishing
P.O. Box 65624
Salt Lake City, UT 84165
www.american-book.com
Printed in the United States of America on acid-free paper.

The Prize

Designed by Stu Smith, design@american-book.com

Publisher's Note: *This is a work of fiction. Names, characters, places, and incidents either are the product of the author's imagination or, are used fictitiously, and any resemblance to actual persons, living or dead, events, or locales is entirely coincidental.*

Library of Congress Cataloging-in-Publication Data is available upon request.

ISBN 1-58982-066-5

LaCourt, M., The Prize

Special Sales

These books are available at special discounts for bulk purchases. Special editions, including personalized covers, excerpts of existing books, and corporate imprints, can be created in large quantities for special needs. For more information e-mail orders@american-book.com or call 1-801-486-8639.

The Prize

A Novel about Bullies and Victims… and What Drives Them

By M. LaCourt

Dedication

I dedicate *The Prize* to my grandchildren:
    Michael Olson
    Brendon Piskula
    Nathan Guggenheim
    Riley Piskula
    Annie Guggenheim
    Jonathan Stone
    Oriane Piskula
    Samuel Hellegers
    Ariel Guggenheim
    Tattiana Piskula
    Sonja Stone
    Maggie Maxstadt
    Mark Allen Stone
    Hannah Hellegers

May they all have prizes.

And to my deceased grandson, Andrew Garrison, who didn't get the opportunity to participate.

Foreword

The Prize is a courageous and compelling story that challenges all the taken-for-granted "truths" about bullies and victims that have proven over and over again to be ineffective in reducing school violence.

The Prize, however, is far more than an exposé of the inadequacies of traditional ideas in the amelioration of bullying. The book offers an inspirational alternative based on two revolutionary ideas. LaCourt takes the very provocative perspective, considered downright dangerous by many, that bullies and victims are co-conspirators—not equal participants, but contributing players—in the tragic cycle of violence, and she considers proactive action by both to be critical. Perhaps even more radical is her abiding faith in these participants, the bullies and the victims, to solve their differences in their own way, without the encumbrances of adult-imposed rules.

The result is not only a refreshing alternative that embraces and enlists the natural resiliency and competencies of youth, but also an entertaining story that is both evocative and delightful to read. I will heartily recommend this book to adolescents and their families, and to anyone desiring a creative perspective that incorporates the voice of youth.

—Barry Duncan, Psy.D.
Co-Director, Institute for the Study of Therapeutic Change (www.talingcure.com),
Co-Author of *The Heroic Client: Doing Client Directed, Outcome Informed Therapy* and *Heroic Clients, Heroic Agencies: Partners for Change*

Preface

I've been a student of cooperation all my life. Striving to understand and promote cooperation between people—that's my mission.

In 1999, shortly after the tragedy at Columbine, my colleagues and I at Communication Programs, LLC, developed a bully prevention program for seventh- and eighth-grade students. Kosciuszko Middle School in Milwaukee, Wisconsin, graciously agreed to host a pilot of our program. Kosciuszko has a culturally and racially mixed student population, and is located in one of Milwaukee's highest crime areas.

The seventh-grade students at Kosciuszko and their teacher taught me a great deal about the dynamics between bullies and victims. Consequently, I was deeply compelled to write a realistic story told from the perspective of both the bullies and the victims as they struggle to find answers to tough questions.

Prologue: March 1951

Sydney Schuster's father had carefully chosen the high school, an Episcopalian school with high academic standards. He paid a handsome tuition to provide a safe haven for his bright and sensitive boy.

A moderately wealthy uncle with a love of sports was the only reason John Murphy could attend Saint Agnes School for Boys. The prestigious institution needed a star athlete, and John needed a sports scholarship for college.

John was the quarterback, the brains of the football team. Just about everybody thought John Murphy was an all-around great guy—everyone, that is, except Sydney Schuster.

*****

Sydney's science teacher, Mrs. Trent, told John Murphy and the others to leave Sydney alone. She scolded them, guilted them, and belittled them. Sydney thanked her for her efforts, but he knew it wouldn't help.

In Mrs. Trent's presence the bullies acted contrite, but as soon as they were out of her sight, Sydney heard them laughing. "What's she gonna do about it, the old busybody?"

Sydney stayed out of sight and listened as John snickered and snorted to the others. "She's told our parents. She's done that already. She's sent her little tattletale messages. What's she gonna do, tell them again?" Their laughter echoed in Sydney's ears long after he lay safe in his bed at night.

Sydney tried to warn the school principal that the violence was escalating. He gave Mr. Johannes specific details, showed him minor cuts and bruises that had been inflicted by John and the others.

"You have to understand," Mr. Johannes told Sydney. "John's a little more physical than you are. You see, they're just having fun with you, boy. They don't mean any harm. Avoid them, Sydney. That's your best defense. If they do any *real* harm, you come and tell me, and I'll have a talk with them."

He patted Sydney on the back as he gently ushered the boy toward the door. "In the meantime, ignore them. Take it from me, my boy. That's the best way to get them to leave you alone."

Sydney's shoulders slouched and his eyes teared as he shuffled out of the principal's office.

Thanks a lot for the advice, Mr. Johannes, he thought. *Ignore them? Yeah, sure. How am I supposed to ignore them when they're beating me up? What should I do, Mr. Johannes? Put my mind somewhere else and let them do what they want with my body? Do you think that will stop John, the animal—the creature—the beast?*

When Sydney was out of Mr. Johannes's hearing range, he sneered. "What do you know, Mr. Johannes? What do you know about what it's like to be me? I could be dead tomorrow. What do you care?"

He left his last class promptly, hoping to make it safely to the parking lot where his father's chauffeur would pick him up and take him to services at his temple. He retrieved his yarmulke from his pocket and took comfort in what it symbolized. He said a silent prayer; then he carefully folded it and tucked it back into its hiding place. *No need to give them grist for the mill,* he thought.

Other boys scurried about their business, retrieving belongings from lockers in a hurry to begin the weekend's activities. Sydney knew they wouldn't intervene when John and Kenny and Russ had their fun with him. The teachers were in a mandatory meeting, and the halls were unmonitored.

The fine-boned, dark-haired boy in his school uniform nervously shuffled from one foot to the other as his eyes darted in all directions. His movements through the halls— the timing of them and the routes he took—were carefully calculated to avoid John Murphy and his two backslapping sidekicks.

*****

Sydney's tormentors huddled in the hallway, discussing their strategy for today's game—but it wasn't football they were talking about.

"Sydney's such a wimp," John sneered as he waited with Russ and Kenny for the first glimpse of their target. "Him with his rich father, a chauffeur in a monkey suit to open doors for him—can you beat that? The snobby little shit!"

"Yeah, John, Sydney's a wimp. He's no fun anymore." Russ turned his head away. "Let's just skip it today."

John's eyes narrowed as he caught sight of Sydney peeking around the corner. With his gaze still on Sydney, he grabbed Russ's arm. "Trust me. I'll figure out something to make it more interesting."

John glanced back at Russ and smirked as Russ nodded. The three boys began their ritualistic laughing and chanting: "Run, Sydney, run." Softly, in unison, they continued: "Go tell Mrs. Trent, Sydney." In falsetto, they mocked him: "Mama's boy, Mama's boy."

Sydney stood stone-still, his gaze fixed on John.

John's heart skipped at the sight of Sydney's eyes, big, round, and glassy, contrasting sharply with his blood-drained face.

John and the others walked toward their victim, three abreast. About a yard in front of Sydney, John grabbed Kenny and Russ by their wrists. "Stop. Don't touch him, you guys."

"Daddy's money can't make you a man, Sydney," John spoke in a calm and quiet voice that belied the adrenaline rushing through his veins.

There was no way Sydney could outrun them, but when they took another step toward him, Sydney ran. Sydney ran, and they slapped their thighs and poked each other's shoulders as they gave their prey his head start. They laughed, and they shouted, "Run, Sydney! Run!"

Then Russ took off toward Sydney. John grabbed Kenny's arm to hold him back and yelled to Russ, "Russ, hold on. Sydney can wait. Come here!"

Russ turned and looked back. "I was just gonna…"

"Never mind, Russ. Come back here!"

Russ grumbled under his breath as he rejoined the other two.

John put his arms around Russ and Kenny's shoulders to form a huddle. "Be patient. He'd have to get past us to get out. He can wait. Listen to me. Let's do something different this time—make it more interesting. We all know we can get Sydney to run. Let's see how *long* we can keep him running. Don't touch him. Just keep him running."

The three exchanged high-fives. "Yes!"

"Let the game begin," John shouted to Kenny and Russ—and Sydney.

Sydney ran up the stairs toward the second floor. John ran past him. Sydney turned and ran the other way—down.

John watched from the top of the steps as Russ tripped Sydney and then offered him a hand up. Sydney took Russ's hand and allowed his tormentor to pull him to his feet.

John shouted, "Nice going, Russ. Keep him running."

The three began the chant again: "Run, Sydney, run!" And Sydney ran.

By now, the school was empty except for the teachers. John, Kenny, and Russ pursued Sydney, blocking every attempt to reach the third floor and the safety of the teacher's lounge. They chased him like cowboys herding the steer to the branding place. They finally routed him to the basement, to the boiler room, where nobody could hear or see them.

Sydney panted, "Out of breath."

When he fell in a heap next to the big furnace, Kenny shouted, "Run! Hey, Sydney, you're no fun anymore. Get up! Get up and run!"

Russ's fists were clenched as he danced around like a boxer sparring with an imaginary opponent. John grabbed Russ by the wrist. "Keep your pants on, Russ. We're not done running him yet."

John grabbed Sydney by the hands and pulled him to his feet, but Sydney's knees buckled, and he went down again. "Come on, Sydney. Fight like a man." John stood with his hands on his hips as he leaned over and spat in Sydney's face.

Kenny was kicking his legs karate-style into the air. A stray kick caught John in the elbow.

"Hey, watch what you're doing." John pushed Kenny away.

Sydney was gasping for air and whimpering. The tears rolled down his cheeks, and snot ran from his nose. John bent down and whispered in Sydney's ear. "Take your time, Sydney. Go ahead and catch your breath. We can wait." When John found the yarmulke in its usual pocket, he put the little cap on Sydney's head. "What a cute little boy in his cute little beanie…"

John stood up and looked down at his victim. Sydney wasn't crying anymore. In fact, he wasn't making any sound at all except for his breathing, which was slow and steady. His face was blank—expressionless—and his eyes looked glassy. The yarmulke was still perched on his head.

Kenny struck the first blow. He gave Sydney's limp body a hard kick in the ribs. John kicked back at Kenny's leg. "Don't touch him, Kenny. I think he's getting his wind back." John was breathing hard.

Kenny extended his hand to Sydney. "Come on, Sydney. Get up. The game's not over." Sydney made no move or sound.

Sydney's vacant eyes seemed to be fixed somewhere in the space past John's shoulder. "Look at me, Sydney!" John kicked him—just a soft little kick to jump-start him. *Fight back, Sydney. Defend yourself, you little wimp. Fight back! Dammit, fight back!*

Kenny grabbed Sydney under his armpits and picked him up. Sydney slumped like a rag-doll. Kenny threw him to John like a hot potato. John tossed him to Russ, and they laughed. Then John started punching him in the ribs while Russ held him.

"Run, dammit! Run!"

No matter what they did to him, they couldn't get a reaction from their victim. Their fists and their feet went on automatic pilot, jabbing and kicking at him. They took turns; first one, then another gave a punch to the ribs, a kick to the groin. Appendages with a mind of their own, or no mind at all—animals instinctually smelling blood.

When he saw the blood coming from Sydney's mouth, John froze with his clenched fist in the air. He didn't remember hitting Sydney in the face. John's first impulse was to flee. *Run, John, run,* he thought. He stepped away from Sydney's bleeding face.

Kenny was still holding Sydney by the shoulders. Russ moved in and punched at the lifeless body until Kenny lost his grip and Sydney slumped to the floor.

"Stop! Stop, you guys!" John screamed. "It's not a game anymore! It's not a game anymore; it's real."

John was trying to calm his own panic and figure out what to do when he saw Russ sway and reel and go down on his knees with his head in his hands. "Is he dead? God, did we kill him?"

"Get hold of yourself, Russ," John shouted. "We gotta keep our heads."

Kenny begged, "Get up, Sydney! Get up, you hear me?" Once again, he grabbed Sydney's shoulders and attempted to get him on his feet. "The game's over. You can go home now. C'mon, Sydney, please, just get up. We'll leave you alone now—honest."

After Kenny let Sydney drop to the floor, John leaned over the limp body and put his ear to Sydney's chest. "His heart's still beating, and he's still breathing."

By this time, Russ was on his feet again. He tugged at John's arm. "I say we get the hell out of here. Nobody saw us do it. They can't prove a thing."

John yelled, "We can't just leave him here like this, Russ. He might die!"

Russ danced from one foot to the other. "We gotta get out of here, you guys!"

"Hold on," Kenny barked. "John's right. We can't leave him here, not like this. We can get out of here, but then we gotta call someone to come get him."

The sweat trickled down Russ's forehead; his whole body twitched as he backed away from his buddies pleading, "OK, OK, you guys, but we don't have to say it was us—we don't have to say who called!"

John checked Sydney for vital signs again. "That won't cut it, Russ. Too many people saw us chasing him. I'll stay here with him, and, Kenny, you go call the police. It'll go easier on us that way. Russ, suit yourself."

By now the school had been vacated for the weekend, and the four boys were locked in. There really wasn't a choice of what to do after all.

It wasn't long before the ambulance and the police arrived. Sydney was transported to the ER, and the other three were taken into juvenile custody.

*****

Sydney Schuster spent the next fifteen years reliving the nightmare of that beating. John, Russ, and Kenny, being juveniles, got off easy: They got probation, and there is no permanent record of their deeds.

Chapter One
Forty-five Years Later
Menomonee Falls, Wisconsin, April 1996

"So, John, what brings me here today?"

John watched with heightened curiosity as his visitor, Sydney Schuster, an impeccably groomed gentleman in an expertly tailored suit, approached his table. John had been anxiously waiting for half an hour. He took a long swig of his Miller Lite before he pushed his chair back, stood up, and extended a hand to Sydney.

Sydney made no move to accept John's offer of civility. "Tell me, John. What brings the bully to ask his victim to drive all the way from Chicago to have lunch at a rinky-dink restaurant in Menomonee Falls?"

John let his hand drop to his side and forced a smile. "I know this place is not up to your usual standard, Sydney. Thanks for coming." John could have chosen a more prestigious restaurant, but he had his reasons for choosing this one.

Sydney turned his back to John, walked over to the rack, and carefully hung his cashmere coat on a hanger before he seated himself. "I'm waiting, John. What brings me here?"

"I'm glad you came, Sydney." John took his seat across from his guest. "To be honest, I didn't think you would. I suppose I'm just as curious about why you came as you are about why I invited you. Let's order lunch. We have a lot to talk about." He motioned to the waitress for a menu.

A disheveled girl with dingy brown hair and dull eyes approached the table. She handed two menus to John, who smiled up at her as he accepted the grease-smudged bill of fare. "Hi, Susie. How are you? How's the baby? Are you working on your GED?"

Susie stood with her hands on her hips. "The baby has a cold." She glared at John as she rattled on. "Her S.O.B. father is on the run again. I got bills to pay. I don't have time for no GED, Father." She pointed to the menu. "The salmon is nice and fresh today, but I don't recommend the creamed cod."

"The salmon it is, then." John smiled at her again before turning back to his guest. "How about you, Sydney? My treat."

"Salmon's fine."

"Bring us a couple more brews, Susie."

"None for me. I'll have water, lots of ice."

Susie picked up the menus and stomped toward the kitchen. "Two salmon specials, a Miller Lite, and water with lots of ice for Father Murphy and his friend at table two," she hollered. "It's break time for me. You take it, Ann. There'll probably be a good tip in it."

Sydney sat with his arms crossed, a sullen look on his face, as John began the speech he'd been rehearsing for the past several days. "Susie was one of ours at St. Joan's. She and Jerry went through the grades together. Typical story—Jerry was a little wild, and Susie was a pushover. She thought she could save Jerry with her goodness. She kept turning the other cheek, and Jerry kept hitting it."

Sydney rolled his eyes back in his head. "Get on with it, John. I didn't come here to listen to you talk about your students."

"They both know she'll take him back. He'll do all right for a while. He'll keep his nose clean, get a job, and go into treatment—all the things she asks him to do. And he'll be real sweet to her."

When the waitress set the plates of steaming hot salmon, peas, and potatoes *au gratin* on the table in front of the two unlikely companions, John immediately picked up his fork and stuffed his mouth with salmon. "Hmm, this is good." He reached for the bread with one hand and waved his fork with the other. "Go ahead, eat, Sydney, before it gets cold." Still chewing, he went on, "Like I was saying…"

Sydney took a sip of water. "Just get on with it."

John carefully placed his fork on the table and frowned. He was determined to finish his story just as he had planned it. "Just about the time she gets her hopes up, he gets tired of her smothering him. The whole thing starts all over again. He picks a fight, makes it sound like it's her fault. He knocks her around, goes straight for the nearest dealer, gets his fix, and runs."

"Get to the point, John."

John blinked. *I thought it was obvious.* "When she lays down like a rug, he just can't resist the temptation to walk on her."

"You brought me here for this? You brought me here to listen to an old man ramble about a couple of kids?"

"Why did you come, Syd?"

"I came because I wanted to get a good look at John Murphy, the bully in a Roman collar."

John flinched at Sydney's words. He knew he was taking the wrong approach when he answered, "Oh, come on, Sydney. You were a wimp. You were asking for it. All we had to do was give you the eye, and you went running off to mama, or Mrs. Trent, or a cop. We're grown men now; you know what I mean." John scraped some potatoes onto his fork.

"No—yes—well, I suppose I did seek help." Sydney cleared his throat. "It wasn't just giving me the eye, you know. You were downright brutal. You ganged up on me!"

"Yeah, Sydney, I know, but you brought out the worst in us. I admit it did get out of hand, but—"

"But! What do you mean, 'but'? There's no 'but' about it! While you three punks were congratulating each other and celebrating your glorious manhood, I was in the hospital with a broken clavicle and three broken ribs!"

"I'm truly sorry, Syd, but—"

"There you go with the 'but' again. You don't seem to understand. It wasn't just *physical* wounds that you inflicted. I was in shock! Do you know how much distress and anguish you and your macho cohorts caused me?"

Sydney slammed his knuckles on the table. "Right now, I feel like giving *you* a few broken bones, John!"

A picture flashed in John's mind: a picture of himself being beaten up in a public place—on his own turf—by Sydney Schuster. Sydney probably could do it. Syd was in better physical condition than John now. *Run, John run*, he thought.

Instead, he said, "Maybe if you had done just that, Sydney—stood up for yourself—if you would have fought back, things might have been different for both of us."

"You're trying to tell me it was *my* own fault? I *made* you do it?" Sydney shook his head. "I'm sorry I came here. You haven't changed, John. I don't think I could begin to make you understand. It took me years of therapy to finally stop the nightmares, the tremors, the anxiety, and the fears. You robbed me! You robbed me of something I can never recoup." Sydney pursed his lips and glared.

John took another long swig of his beer as he let Sydney's words roll around in his head. "All right, Sydney, I get the point. Me and Kenny and Russ ganged up on you; we beat the crap out of you, broke some bones, and put you in a hospital. We were *kids*. We didn't understand the emotional trauma we put you through. I'm truly sorry for what we did. You're right. We acted like animals; we smelled blood, and we went for the jugular."

Sydney's placidity invited John to continue.

The priest's voice was gentle as he risked making his point again. "I'm not trying to make excuses. There is no excuse for that kind of violence—but I don't think we robbed you of anything. I think there was a certain something you never had in the first place. I'm not trying to excuse or dismiss what we did, but you did ask for it, Sydney."

John held his breath. *This is all wrong,* he thought. *I didn't mean for it to go this way.* He watched the veins in Sydney's red face throb.

Sydney stood up, put both hands on the table, and leaned into John's face. In a guttural voice, he hissed, "I don't have to take this from you."

John sat motionless. He peered straight ahead, not daring to utter another syllable.

When Sydney turned and moved toward the door, John breathed a little easier. In desperation, he thought, *Thank God, he's not going to get violent. There may still be a chance to explain. I can't let him go.*

He sprang to his feet and blocked Sydney's exit. *Play it cool; be gentle,* he warned himself as he grabbed Sydney's sleeve. "Come on, Sydney." He spoke softly now, almost in a whisper. "We're forty years past all that. We're grown men, not adolescent boys. I'm a priest now, not a smart-ass bully. I'm sure the years have changed you as well."

John tightened his grip on Sydney's sleeve. "Come on, Syd, sit down. Listen to me. I think we want the same thing. There are boys like Jerry and girls like Susie who are struggling with some of the very same things that got us off on the wrong foot."

Sydney made no move to leave. John tenaciously kept his hold on Sydney's sleeve.

John felt the inquisitive eyes of four other diners and two waitresses on him. He looked out the window to where

Chapter One

Sydney's chauffeur was waiting. He glanced at their table, where the half-eaten food and the crumpled napkins had been abandoned.

Sydney shook John's hand off his sleeve, stared John straight in the face for a moment, turned, walked back to the table, and sat down.

John let out an unconsciously held breath and followed Sydney back to the table.

"Let's get this straight, John. I was the victim then; Susie's the victim now. She didn't ask for it any more than I did. Surely Jerry has committed a crime or two. He should be in jail. Where are the police when he beats her up? Anyway, I'm assuming you didn't invite me here to talk about Susie and Jerry. Get to the point."

"Susie and Jerry *are* the point, Syd. Let me ask you, what good did it do you to go to the authorities when you were being victimized?"

"They weren't much help," Sydney responded in a monotone.

"You damn well know they weren't. Look, Syd, I'm not proud of what we did to you, but I gotta believe I'm a decent human being. I asked you here because I want you to help me help the Susies and the Jerrys. There's gotta be a better way—"

"I might look like a patsy to you, John, but one thing I've learned: I can't just keep giving money to every cause that comes along with its hand out." Sydney pushed his chair back from the table and folded his arms across his chest. "What happens in the wealthiest families is no different from what you just described."

John folded his hands as if to pray. "I was hoping—"

"Believe me," Sydney barked, "all the money in the world can't transform a bully into a decent human being!"

John winced. "I was hoping you'd help us to keep our parish school open. There are a lot of kids who need our help. It's the weak ones I worry about the most."

In spite of how badly he thought things had gone, John was determined to put the period at the end of his prepared speech. "They're the ones who need a no-nonsense school where they can learn to be winners in a tough, competitive world."

"You have a lot of nerve, John asking me, of all people!"

"I knew it was a long shot. The board's already voted to close our school. The pay is so bad we can't attract good teachers. There are only two nuns left, and they're too old and out-of-sync with the times."

"Let me see if I understand you." Sydney shook his finger at John and spoke through clenched teeth. "You want *me* to give you money so you can keep pumping out more little do-gooder Catholic girls like Susie and more little bullies for the Susies to take care of. Just tell me, John, just tell me how do you expect *that* to help?"

"I don't know, Syd." John looked down at his empty plate and drew a deep breath. "I guess you're right. What we're doing isn't working."

In a whisper, he continued, "Every time I look into Susie's eyes or see Jerry's face at mass, I feel so sad and guilty for having failed them. I pray to my Lord for guidance, and I keep hearing the voice of Jesus, and His holy mother Mary saying, 'Listen to the children.'" John shook his head. "I just can't give up on them."

"John, maybe you ought to take a lesson from your own good book. Accept that which you cannot change. I'm not a religious man, but at least I've learned that much."

"I can't do that, Syd." John put his elbows on the table and supported his head between his hands. "I can't give up."

Sydney drew his chair closer to the table. "Listen to me, John. My wife and I gave our sons our best. We did everything according to the book. We read to them. We played with them. We taught them to share their toys, to say I'm sorry, to make amends, to be charitable to those less fortunate."

John lifted his head from its resting place between his hands. He leaned forward, looked into Sydney's eyes, and listened without comment. The circumstances—the details—were different, but Sydney sounded like so many other sad parents who'd done their best.

"We didn't just send them to temple; we went as a family," Sydney spoke softly. "We took them around the world, and not just to the Riviera, either. They saw Africa and India. They saw poverty—real poverty. We wanted them to have compassion for others and to appreciate their own good fortune."

"You were a good father, Syd. You have to believe that."

"When my wife died, I didn't try to replace her by marrying another mother for them—I *became* their mother. I did everything for them."

Sydney's voice took on a sarcastic edge as he continued. "I wanted them to feel good about themselves. Well, I succeeded in getting them to feel good about themselves, all right—perhaps a little too good. After all my efforts, I'm sad to say that my sons are bullies. They care only about themselves. And there's not a thing I can do about it. I've learned to accept that which I cannot change."

"I'm sorry for you, Syd…for you and your boys."

"I'm sorry for their victims."

"So, where do we go from here, Sydney?"

"I guess you go looking for another angel, and I go looking for a meaningful way to spend my fortune so there will be less of it for my sons to badger people with after I'm dead. Thanks for lunch, John."

"You haven't eaten, Syd."

"I wasn't hungry."

Chapter Two
Karter Goes to School Today
Milwaukee, Wisconsin, April 1996

Karter Johnson tugged at the collar of his jacket, pulling it tight around his neck and his hunched-up shoulders as he scurried down the street past the crack house and the storefront church. *There ain't gonna be nobody on the streets today. Might just as well go to school*, he thought.

He ducked in the doorway of the Kwik-Mart, glanced at the familiar sign in the window: No Students Allowed. He pulled a cigarette from the pack in his pocket and lit up, took a long drag. When he saw the clerk inside close the register and move toward the door, Karter scowled, tossed the cigarette on the sidewalk, and looked at his watch.

Damn, I'm late. I'll have to stand outside and wait until that witch decides to get off her fat black ass and let me in. She'll pretend she doesn't hear the buzzer, or that it's broken, or that she's deep in thought, while she pores over some Mickey Mouse thing on her desk. Then when she's damn good and ready, she'll look toward the door and squint her eyes. She'll make believe she doesn't know me. She's a mean S.O.B. People like her shouldn't be in charge of others. Whatever—I gotta get in out of this frickin rain.

The lightning flashed, and the thunder boomed loud enough to make Karter jittery. Even so, he hesitated as he contemplated the building across the street.

The school was built in the 1930s with depression monies—red-orange brick with boring gray mortar, mimicking the European architecture of a century past. Instead of being flanked with formal gardens like its continental predecessor, the building's grounds were smothered with asphalt and concrete. The playgrounds and the parking lots were fenced with eight-foot-high chain links and locked—inaccessible without the requisite pass.

He'd have used a different entrance if he could, but there was no other way in. The wind blew fiercely, and Karter shivered as he darted up the steps to the door.

Buzz, buzz, buzz. Bang, bang. "Dammit, let me in. It's cold out here," he shouted.

The hall monitor, a heavy-set woman in jeans and a "Woman Power" sweatshirt, ambled to the entrance. She peered out the window before unlocking the door. "Oh, it's you, Karter. You're late again."

Karter pushed her aside. "Just let me in and mind your own business."

As Karter strode to the familiar desk at the end of the hall, the monitor followed. She shoved a pencil and a clipboard at him. "Any weapons besides your bad mouth, your bad breath, and your 'my-farts-don't-stink' attitude?"

Chapter Two

Karter signed in and threw the clipboard down on the desk. "Just give me my pass."

She waved the pass in the air. "This will only get you as far as the office, jerk."

"Witch."

"What's that you say, Karter?"

"Just gimme my pass."

Karter grabbed the pink slip and traipsed down the hall as the monitor called out, "You better learn some respect!" When he was out of her sight, he gave her the finger and mumbled more obscenities.

The halls of the school were wide, well lit, and covered with posters. Some were in Spanish, some in languages Karter didn't know, and some in English. They all carried warnings about dangers: dangers of drugs, dangers of sex, and dangers of dropping out of school. Karter smirked as he sauntered past them.

When he ambled into the office, the woman behind the counter covered the mouthpiece of the phone. "Be with you in a minute, Karter." She motioned for him to sit on the bench.

"Take your time, Mrs. Sherman. I got nothin better to do." He took his wet jacket off, shook it, and tossed it on the bench. *Sure could use a cigarette*, he thought.

When Mrs. Sherman hung up the phone, she turned to Karter. "You're late again, Karter." She sighed, shrugged her shoulders, and rolled her eyes. "You know the routine. You'll have to wait here until the change of classes before you can go to your designated destination. Do you have a book you can read or an assignment you can do while you wait?"

What the hell is she talking about, designated destination? Why can't people just talk plain English?

"Yeah, sure."

Karter sat on the bench and stared vacantly into space. He fidgeted and stretched. Twenty minutes passed. He still had the rain in his bones. He needed to move. When the bell finally rang, he bolted out of the office.

Down the hall, several kids waved and gave him high-fives. As he approached a group of Hispanic girls, Karter gave Theresa Torres a pat on the butt in passing. He knew he was taking a chance; if he were caught, it would be an automatic suspension. He knew Theresa would keep her mouth shut, though. She liked it. He looked back to exchange smiles with her.

Karter reached the classroom just in time to hear Mr. Beemers say, "OK, in your seats, everybody. Notebooks out. Start writing. The questions are on the board."

Mr. Beemers paced as he talked loud enough to be heard over the commotion of thirty students getting settled into their seats. "Quiet down now. We have work to do."

As usual, about a fourth of those enrolled were absent. He handed out pencils and paper to students who came unprepared—approximately half the class. "Write the questions and then your answers. When you're done, we'll have discussion time."

Karter raised his hand and asked, "Why do we have to write the questions?" He grinned. "Couldn't we just write the answers—just for a little change in the routine?"

His classmates laughed. Karter shrugged his shoulders and made with the big eyes as he scanned the group. "Why do more work than we have to?"

The class laughed again—this time, harder. They would use any excuse to break the routine; to stall long enough to avoid the discussion; to never have to admit, "I don't know."

Mr. Beemers rapped on his desk to get their attention. "Well now, class, I'll just be collecting those papers at the end of the hour. You wouldn't want *me* to have to work too hard, would you? I'll need to know if your answers match my questions. Won't I?"

Most heads had been bent over their papers for a few minutes when Mr. Beemers spoke again. "Karter, I notice you're not writing. What's the problem?"

"My lead broke."

The class laughed again.

"Well, go and sharpen your pencil, boy. You're not helpless."

Karter slid out of his seat and ever so slowly sauntered to the pencil sharpener, taking the opportunity for a stretch and a few words with his friends along the way.

Mr. Beemers cleared his throat. "If you don't have time to finish in class, Karter, you can come in after school. I'll be available for any help you might want then."

Karter got back to his desk and began writing on the piece of paper his teacher had provided. "Question number one," he wrote, "who needs this crap?"

Mr. Beemers was still pacing. "Does anybody need more time to prepare for the discussion?"

A few hands went up—the hands of the slackers, the smart alecks, and the slow ones. They wouldn't finish no matter how much time they got.

"Then let's get started." He looked for open faces. Karter kept his eyes down.

"Mohandas, will you read the first question out loud for the class?"

Mohandas—Moe to his classmates—looked at the board and read, "Who wrote the second amendment to the Constitution?" Moe stood respectfully and shifted from one foot to the other. "I am not certain that I am understanding the question, Mr. Beemers."

"What is it that you don't understand, Mohandas?"

"The writing of the second amendment to the Constitution occurred through a process involving a very large number of men. There were many versions before one could be agreed upon."

"You're absolutely correct. Good thinking."

Mr. Beemers reached into the bag he kept in his desk drawer, took out a candy bar, and tossed it to Moe.

Karter exchanged a knowing look with his buddies. They had Moe pegged for the class brown-nose. They didn't hate him or anything like that—just thought he was a little pathetic.

"Eduardo Cortez," Mr. Beemers called out as he looked at a list of students from the roster on his desk. "Can you name one of the men involved in the writing of the second amendment to the Constitution?"

Karter watched as his friend sat frozen in his seat, eyes down. *Poor Eddie. Beemers knows better than to call on me. He wouldn't want me to get them laughing again.*

"On your feet, boy. Stand up when I call on you."

Still looking down at his desk, Eddie shuffled to his feet slowly, but said nothing.

"Well, boy, come on. I asked you a question. If you don't know the answer, have the courage to say so."

Eddie mumbled, "I don't know." Nobody laughed.

"All right, Eddie, you can sit down. Does anyone know the answer?"

The Stein twins, Jenna and Becca, rolled their eyes in unison. The girls, who were always together, were recent transfers from a fancy private school. Karter was curious about them. He'd heard rumors of a family tragedy. *Those two don't belong in a class like this—in a school like this. That's for sure!*

Mr. Beemers continued to lead the discussion with the few students who seemed genuinely interested. He let the others be.

Karter and his buddies had no stake in Mr. Beemer's agenda. They sat in the back of the room whispering about Maria Guliano. They took bets on whether she would put out. Eddie said she'd be a pushover, Demon thought she'd put up a fight, and Karter was convinced she'd like the attention.

Tashina Jones stomped over to where the boys were sitting and shouted at them. "You boys leave dat girl alone. She ain't no ho! You watch how you be talkin bout her." Her nostrils flared as she glared at them.

Eddie pointed a finger at her and snickered mischievously. "Look at you, Tashina. You jealous we ain't talking about you? You want some too?"

Karter's eyes sparkled as he laughed. "Meet you later, little chocolate girl."

Tashina stood her ground with her hands on her hips and her feet firmly planted; she raised one eyebrow as she dared them. "You boys know better than to mess wit Tashina Jones. You mess wit me, and I bite you balls."

Maria turned around from her seat in front of them. She tugged at Tashina's jeans and whispered, "Never mind, Tashina. They don't mean any harm. They're just talking."

Mr. Beemers walked to the back of the room. "All right, all right, break it up. What's going on here?"

Maria stood up. "It's OK, Mr. Beemers; just a little misunderstanding."

The others kept their mouths shut and their eyes averted.

Mr. Beemers was instructing them to separate when the bell rang. They all made a dash for the door.

Tashina fell into step with her friend. Karter walked quietly behind to eavesdrop.

"You better watch out for em, Maria. They be up to no good. Take it from me, girl. You gots to learn to stand up for yourself."

"Yeah, I know, but they scare me. I see them looking at me and I freeze. I think I'd just better do what they say."

"Girl, you jus stick by me. I ain't lettin you outta my sight til you learns to fight!"

"Maybe I should talk to Mr. Beemers. Maybe he could do something."

"Come on, girl. You know better than dat. What *he* gonna do?"

"Mr. Beemers is a nice guy, Tashina. I like him. He's one of the few teachers who cares about us. He even runs an AA group for kids on his own time."

"Dat don't cut nothin. Not wit the likes a Karter Johnson and his dimwit stooges. They jus get mad when they finds out you been rattin on em, and they wait 'til no one's round to protec ya. Then what ya gonna do? No, you jus stick by me, girl. I ain't afraid to fight em, and they knows it. They won't touch you wit me around."

"They don't mean any harm, Tashina. They just talk big."

Karter decided it was time to have a little fun with the girls. He brushed past them, turned his head, and winked. "I wouldn't count on it, Maria." He had a devilish look in his eye. "I'll see you later, little chocolate girl."

*****

After school, Tashina insisted on walking Maria safely to her door. "What you do, girl? You look like you alla time in a hurry to get home."

"I have to get supper started and keep an eye on my little brother and sister."

"They sure be trainin you right."

"What do you mean?"

"A woman's place is in the home, takin care a the men and the children."

"I don't mind. At least it's safe there."

"How come you mama ain't there doin woman's work?"

"My mom works in my dad's body shop. She takes care of all the customers."

"She be takin care a her man?"

"Mom says if she wasn't there, he'd be so busy having a good time with his beer-drinking buddies that he'd forget to collect the fees. Somebody's got to tend to the practical things."

"They be teachin you your place. What they be teachin you brother? What he gotta do?"

"Rick's a guy. He doesn't have to do much of anything. Since he got his license and the car dad fixed up for him, he's gone all the time. That's fine with me."

Tashina watched her friend unlock the door and enter the house before she left. She shook her head as she walked away. *Dat girl, she be askin for a whole lot a trouble in this here life, and she don't even know it.*

Tashina headed for her mother's storefront shop across the street from the George Webb restaurant that her grandmother managed. She pulled up a stool next to the worktable, where Mama was hovering over a customer's tax return. As usual, she reveled in telling her mama the stories of the day.

"I tol dat white boy, he mess wit me and I bite his balls!"

"Ha ha! Tashina, you said that? You tell them like it is, girl. You give them back twice what they dish out."

When she'd finished laughing, Mama put the paper she was working on to the side and hugged her daughter. "That's my girl, Tashina. You did good. Nobody walks on Shanita Jones' daughter."

Chapter Two

"You taught me good, Mama, you and Grandma. Us Jones women don't need no man to do our biddin. We takes care a ourselves. And we don't let no man push our buttons, neither."

"You learn good, girl."

The counter was strewn with tax law books open to various pages and stacks of returns waiting to be opened. Tashina glanced at the chaos. "We gonna eat at Grandma's restaurant again tonight, Mama?"

"Looks that way, sweetie. You mind?"

"Nah, Grandma treats us special."

"That's cause we are special, honey."

*****

The rain stopped and the sun came out. Karter, Demon, and Eddie shot hoops at the neighborhood playground, just like half the days since they met in kindergarten. They bantered about what it would be like to have Maria all to themselves—all of them at once, that is.

They had no real intention to act out their fantasies. The macho talk was meant to make them feel powerful and important—in each other's eyes.

Demon was the first to leave. "Gotta go, guys. I promised I wouldn't be late for dinner. Gotta keep the old lady happy if you want peace in the house. That's what my dad always says, anyway. See ya."

Eddie passed the ball to Karter so hard it nearly knocked Karter off-balance. "Hey, take it easy. What'd I ever do to you?" He tossed the ball back to Eddie.

"Oh, it's nothing, Karter." Eddie sat on the curb with the basketball in his hands. "I just don't feel like going home. A restaurant ain't no kind of home. You know how it is. They got me busing the tables every damn night—cleaning up tacos and enchiladas. The sloppy customers don't give a damn where they drop 'em."

"I don't want to go home any more than you do." Karter sat down next to Eddie. "My old man's on the road, and my ma's got her hands full with the retard and the pansy brat."

"My pa's got my little sister washing dishes and cleaning vegetables. Mama don't talk to Pa. Pa's always complaining about how sick he is." Eddie groaned. "I'll take the lecture and the grounding. It won't stick, anyway."

Karter put his arm around his friend's shoulder. "Let's go find some action. Got any cash on ya?"

"Not enough for a pack of cigarettes, but enough for a coke." Eddie tossed the ball on the ground. "Let's go."

The two boys, their oversized shirts hanging down past their butts and their raggedy pant legs dragging in the dirt, put a bounce in their steps as they headed for the coke machine outside the Kwik-Mart.

"Hey, Eddie, what do you think of those two new girls?"

"You mean the Stein twins?"

"Yeah."

"A couple of rich-brat snobs if you ask me. I can't figure out what they're doing in a school like this."

"They used to go to a private school. Jewish Day School or something like that. I heard their mother tried to kill herself."

"Really?"

"Yeah, left the motor running with the garage door closed."

"Coulda been an accident."

"That's not the way I heard it."

"Hey, look, there's Rick Guliano."

"Hey, Rick—wait up. Give us a ride?"

They caught up to him just as Rick was getting into his car.

"Hey, punks, what are you up to? Hurry up, get in. I ain't got all day."

The two climbed onto the front seat next to Rick. Eddie asked, "Hey, Rick, got any dope?"

Rick gunned the motor. "Hey, Eddie, got any bread?"

Chapter Three
Reciprocity
Chicago, Illinois, May 1996

The shrill sounds of his own screams woke him up. The damp sheets were twisted around his shivering body. Sydney looked at the clock at his bedside. Three A.M., it blinked at him. *Still there, are you? I'd thought I'd done with you—damn!* He untangled himself from the sheets, got up, and headed for the shower.

He sat in the dark for hours before Kevin turned the light on. "You're up early this morning, sir."

"Couldn't sleep. How about some coffee, Kevin?"

Sydney sipped his French roast black and ate his simple breakfast: one poached egg, a slice of hearty sourdough bread, a scoop of fresh mozzarella, and imported, vine-ripened tomato with fresh basil.

Kevin moved quietly and gracefully as he tidied the house. Sydney was grateful for the affability of his all-around manservant and chauffeur.

When he'd finished his meal, Sydney settled into his soft, Italian leather chair and peered out the window of his penthouse apartment on Chicago's prestigious East Side. He looked at the colorful sailboats on the lake without really seeing them. His *New York Times* sat neatly folded on the sparkling chrome and glass-top table to his right.

"Kevin, come here. Sit down. Talk to me."

"Sir?"

"Put the tray down and come here. The dishes can wait. Pour yourself some coffee. "

Kevin poured his own coffee and freshened Sydney's cup before he sat down.

"Do you have a cigarette, Kevin?"

"You don't usually smoke, sir." Kevin reached in his pocket for his pack.

"No, but I'd like one now, if you have one."

Kevin tapped the pack, offered his boss a cigarette, and lit it for him.

"Go ahead, Kevin. Have one yourself."

"That's all right, sir. I'll get an ashtray."

Kevin returned with the ashtray and sat down again.

Sydney puffed awkwardly. "I have this nagging question," he said. "Does survival of the fittest mean that bullies survive best?"

"It would certainly seem that way, sir."

"Hitler's dead, but his ideas survive today. When one bully dies, there's always another to take his place. It seems the sickness gets passed on from generation to generation. Do bullies pass on their tendency for violence to their progeny?"

"I'm certain some traits get passed through our genes, sir."

Sydney made a face and snuffed his cigarette out in the ashtray. "Are the strong ones, the most aggressive of us, hell-bent on destroying the weak ones—the gentler ones—to ensure their own survival?"

Kevin fidgeted in his chair. "I'm not exactly an expert on Darwin, sir, but I don't think that's what he meant."

"Oh, stop. Stop with the 'sir' stuff and just talk to me, Kevin."

"Well, sir—I mean, well, as far as I understand it, Darwin wasn't talking about the most aggressive individuals when he used the word 'fit.' I don't think he meant 'fittest.' He wasn't necessarily referring to a person's individual traits. He was, I think, talking about a complementary fitting between species and their environment. We're all part of each other's environment after all, aren't we, sir?"

"Are you saying the word 'fit' should be 'fitting'—a gerund and not an adjective?"

"I think so. When the term 'fit' is used as a noun, it means the fit between us—not a person. Some people use the term 'fittest,' and I believe they do mean to refer to the specific characteristics of an individual. I've read some on the subject."

Sydney listened with heightened interest as Kevin continued. "With regard to the part about fitting, for example, several bird species live on or near large mammals. The mammals could easily destroy the pesky little things, or at least shoo them away, but they don't."

"Why not?"

"The birds eat the insects off the mammals."

"The mammals let the birds live because they're useful to them?"

"It's more than that. They're useful to each other."

"How so?"

Kevin settled back in his chair. "I believe I will have that cigarette, sir, if you don't mind."

"That's quite all right. Go ahead."

"Take the Cape buffalo and the oxpecker, for example." Kevin poured more coffee. "As I was saying, the oxpecker eats the insects off the buffalo. Insect bites are a threat to the buffalo because they carry diseases that are potentially harmful. The buffalo provides shelter and food for the birds."

Sydney squinted. "Go on."

"The buffalo and the bird derive reciprocal benefit. It's the same with the cowbird and the cow. In a sense, they cooperate with each other and put up with minor inconveniences in the best interest of their own selfish need to survive."

"So what you're saying is that our survival depends on how well we get along with each other. You scratch my back, and I scratch yours? Something like that?"

"I'm no scholar, but that's what I think."

"But why should I scratch your back? How will I know you won't just take my favor and give nothing in return?"

"Because we need each other." Kevin took a long drag of his cigarette and put it out.

Chapter Three

"So you're telling me what Darwin meant by survival of the fittest was that those who cooperate for mutual benefit are more likely to survive over time. Is that it then?"

"Yes. Still, there are certain tendencies or traits that are passed on genetically. I'm not quite sure I understand that part very well."

"I suppose you could say those who develop a knack for getting along with their environment live longer and healthier. They produce healthier offspring, and more of them."

"That's how I understand it."

When Sydney took another sip of his cold coffee and made a nasty face, Kevin made a move toward the kitchen. "Let me get some fresh coffee, sir."

"Yes, do."

When Kevin returned, Sydney was pacing. Kevin poured more coffee and placed two small croissants on the table, and the two men settled down to resume their conversation.

Sydney began. "There's this young man—name of Jerry. He's a bully. I don't think he's surviving any better than the wife he bullies."

"What do you mean?"

"Jerry blames Susie, and their child, for his meager lot in life. Then he feels justified for escaping into the drugs that pull him deeper into a hopeless existence."

"What about Susie?"

"They cooperate with each other in a funny sort of way. It's not working for either of them."

"I don't quite understand. They *cooperate* with one another?"

"Yes. He beats her up. She feels like a martyr when she turns the other cheek—and attempts to rescue him."

"But why does he beat her up in the first place?"

"She lets him."

"She lets him?"

Sydney grimaced, trying to ignore the sick feeling in his stomach before he spoke again. "She lays down like a rug and, well, sort of invites him to walk on her." He threw his arms in the air. "It's obvious the law's no help."

Kevin had a puzzled expression on his face. "So they fit with each other in an odd sort of way. They cooperate with each other, yet neither is surviving very well."

"That's what I think John Murphy was trying to tell me. There's a pattern. They're pulling each other down."

"That's a sad story, sir."

"I always thought it was something inside of people that made them bullies, but I guess it's a process, not a thing. It's not what's in us; it's what's *between* us. It's how we behave toward one another."

Sydney gazed out the window again. John Murphy's words echoed in his ears: *We didn't take anything from you. It wasn't there to begin with. You brought out the worst in us.*

"It could go the other way, too."

"What's that you say, Kevin?"

"It could go the other way, too."

"What do you mean?"

"If they can drag each other down, couldn't they just as well drag each other up?"

"Bingo!" Sydney jumped out of his chair and paced again, faster than before. "If the fit between two people can spiral them down into the destruction of both, why can't it work the other way around? A different kind of fit could result in an upward spiral, where both could thrive."

Sydney caught the look of satisfaction on Kevin's face. "Thank you, Kevin. You have no idea how much you've helped me. You scratched my back. I'll scratch yours. Take the rest of the day off. I'll clean up here."

"Thank you, sir."

After Kevin left, Sydney sat pondering quietly for a few more moments. *There's got to be a better way.* He fished the phone number he'd been carrying around for three weeks out of his wallet, and dialed the number.

"St. Joan's rectory, Father John speaking," the voice on the other end came through.

"John, John Murphy?"

"Yes, who's calling?"

"This time, lunch is on me. You'll have to come to Chicago. How about today? Can you make it at one o'clock today?"

"Sydney? Sydney Schuster? Is that you? Well, yes, I suppose I could. It's short notice. I'd have to cancel some appointments. What's up?"

"Never mind, I'll tell you at lunch. Meet me at the Four Seasons Lounge. It's off the lobby in the Four Seasons Hotel on Chestnut, right behind Bloomingdale's. You'll find it. One o'clock sharp."

"OK, I guess I can do that."

"Wait, don't hang up. Did you find an angel to keep your school going?"

"No, unfortunately I haven't, but I'm still trying."

"Well, stop trying right now."

"Does this mean you've changed your mind?"

"No—yes—sort of. I haven't changed my mind. Just be here. I'll tell you at lunch. And by the way, John, you mentioned a convent next to the school. Is it vacant?"

"There are two sisters still living there, but they're going to be relocated to a retirement home by the end of the school year."

"Fine. Keep it that way."

Sydney hung up before John had a chance to respond, then he called Kevin to get him a notebook and a pen. When he realized he'd given Kevin the day off, he went to the desk and got them himself. *Guess I'll have to take a cab to the restaurant.*

He wrote, "Ask the children??? You want answers? Ask the children! Both the bullies and the victims!" He underlined the last part three times and wrote those six words again. He pushed his chair back, took a deep breath, and thought, *If they could work it out for themselves—if they had to work it out for themselves, how would they do it?*

"Sydney Schuster," he shouted to the air, "you have a mission!" He turned on the stereo and sang exuberantly along with the music. He danced and clicked his heels as he loaded the dishwasher and wiped the counters.

*****

52

Chapter Three

Upon seeing the commotion at the restaurant reservation desk, Sydney motioned to the headwaiter to approach his table. "What's the problem, Michael?"

"You know the rules, sir. No tie, no service. I can't break the rules, even for you."

"He's a priest. He doesn't wear ties. He wears collars."

"He's not wearing either at the moment, sir."

"So just give him a tie, for God's sake."

"I was about to offer one when you called me over."

"Problem solved."

Sydney handed the *New Yorker* he'd been reading to the waiter. "Dispose of this for me, would you please."

Sydney stifled a laugh as John adjusted the borrowed tie around the collar of a knit pullover. He stood and offered his hand. "Thanks for coming, John. Sit down."

"Sorry, Syd. If I'd have known, I would have worn one—a tie, I mean. I do have one, you know."

"A collar would have been fine."

"Sorry I'm late, too. I got a little turned around."

The waiter poured a bit of wine into Sydney's glass. Sydney twirled the glass to coat the sides with the deep red liquid. He smelled first, sipped, and swished it around in his mouth. "This will be fine."

John sipped his wine, smiled, and raised his glass. "You have good taste, Sydney."

"Yes, I do."

The waiter put the bottle on the table. "May I take your order, sir?"

Sydney waved the menu away. "Just bring the *carte du jour* for me." He folded and unfolded his napkin impatiently while John pondered the bill of fare. He had forgotten how overwhelming the menu could be to inexperienced diners.

"I'll have the garlic-herbed lamb chops, shiitake mushrooms, and risotto Florentine." John handed the menu to the waiter. "Oh, and some of your liver paté for the bread, please." He reached for his wine. "So why did you call me, Syd?"

"Be patient, John, I'll get to it. How many rooms in the convent?"

"Twelve."

"What's the layout?"

"Like a dorm. The rooms are small, meant for single occupancy. There are two common rooms for socializing, a kitchen, and a dining hall."

"Is the school equipped with computers?"

"No."

"Does it have a gym?"

"Yes."

"A cafeteria?"

"No, the children go home for lunch."

"What's the town like? Are there any blacks? Hispanics? Other ethnic groups? Is it safe for minority kids on the streets?"

When their entrées arrived, Sydney was surprised and slightly annoyed by the interruption. John, on the other hand, put his nose close to his plate and took in the aromas. "Thank you, Syd. This is a nice treat."

"My pleasure, John."

Chapter Three

Sydney watched as John delved into his entrée without the slightest hesitation. John shoveled and chewed and uttered sounds of delight between mouthfuls.

Sydney picked at his food and pondered his guest. *He sounds like he's having an orgasm. How can the man eat with such incredible abandonment? He's totally oblivious to everything but the food on his plate.*

When John had consumed every morsel, he dabbed at his chin, wiped his hands, and placed the crumpled napkin on the table. "What are you up to, Syd?"

Sydney pushed his half-full plate aside. *Is he going to clean my plate, too?* Sydney hesitated for a moment before he poured more wine. *No, I guess he's finished now.*

"I've been giving a lot of thought to what you said during our last conversation, John. You challenged me with a whole different way to evaluate my life—not just what happened, but my very identity. You may not know it, but you changed me."

"Phew, that sounds pretty profound." John wiped his forehead with his napkin.

"You showed me that I played a part in my own victimization. That was a bitter pill for me to swallow, but you made your point."

"I'm glad you told me. But you could have told me that on the phone. What's going on, Syd?"

"What was life like for you, John, when you were young?"

John lifted his glass toward Sydney and smiled. "I was good-looking, robust, and fun-loving—and an outstanding athlete. Women were attracted to me. I could have married many times—came close once."

Sydney left his glass on the table. "As I recall, you were pretty aggressive. Were you born that way?"

John put his glass down without drinking. "I'll admit I wasn't a saint. I drove fast cars and ran with a tough and rowdy crowd. I broke a few laws, and I was fast on my way toward some serious crime—I could just as well have ended up spending my life in prison as in the priesthood. I made the better choice in the nick of time."

He seems like an honest and forthright fellow. I think I could even like him. "Ever got lonely?"

"I have my families—three hundred of them. They need me."

Sydney hesitated for a moment. "I know you want to keep your school open—and you've admitted you don't have all the answers."

"I'm listening, Syd." John's eyes were wide.

"You said, 'Listen to the children,' didn't you?"

"What are you getting at, Syd?"

"Maybe we should ask them."

"Go on."

"What do you think would happen if we, the adults, got out of their way? We put a group of kids together in a boarding school with a challenge to work things out for themselves. Would your church be amenable to renting the school and the convent to a non-religious entity?"

"Hold on, Syd." John held the palms of his hands toward Sydney. "They need our guidance. We can't just throw a bunch of kids together without supervision. They'd kill each other. They'd bring on the drugs and have orgies. Syd, I know kids. It would never work."

"You said it yourself," Sydney challenged. "Relying on the authorities never worked for me—and you were right!"

"My board would never go for it. My families wouldn't go for it. My bishop wouldn't allow it. There's no way on God's green earth that the parents of St. Joan's would allow their children to be unsupervised around the clock from Monday through Friday." John was breathing hard and talking fast.

"Slow down, John. I'm not talking about your kids—I'm not talking about a school that makes God and religion the central focus—the all-consummate authority. I'm talking about the real world where people encounter others who don't necessarily think like them, look like them, or act like them—some of them don't even believe there is a God."

John was quick to rebut. "That's the problem. Kids today aren't getting the spiritual guidance they need."

Sydney was counting on the fact that John was deeply disturbed about his school's failure to help Susie and Jerry. "Your track record at St. Joan's isn't so good, John."

John flinched. The waiter interrupted with the dessert menu before John had a chance to respond.

Sydney passed on dessert. "I'll just have an espresso."

John accepted the menu, and Sydney thought, *How could he possibly think of food at a time like this? I just insulted the man, and he sits there reading the menu.*

John ordered the chocolate cheese torte with raspberry sauce and coffee with cream and sugar.

After his order was taken, John shot the questions without waiting for answers. "Where would you get the kids? Why would their parents agree to such a thing? How could you guarantee that these kids would be safe, and who would take the fall if it didn't work? I just can't see it, Sydney. You can't just throw a bunch of kids together and hope for the best." John folded his arms across his chest.

"I haven't got all the details worked out yet, John. I'm thinking in terms of some external incentive to motivate them to cooperate with each other." Sydney sat back and waited for a response.

"Hmm. Sounds like an awfully big risk to me."

Sydney gambled on another gibe. "What you're doing isn't working."

John gave his host a stern look. "You sure like to point that out, Syd."

Sydney cocked his head. "Well?"

John stood up and put his hands on the back of his chair. "Where would you see me fitting into this grand plan of yours—I mean besides getting the church board to agree to let you rent the school and the convent?"

"John, read my lips. I can get buildings anywhere I choose. It's not about the facility. It's you I need. Sit down; you're making me nervous."

John resumed his place at the table. "OK, say more."

"It was your idea to listen to the kids. If they succeed, we have to have a way to figure out just what they did that made it work, and if they fail, we have to learn why. I want you to help me work out the details and to be there, watching and learning from the kids."

"You want the kids to work things out for themselves, right? And I'm just supposed to watch? Syd, I couldn't just sit by and let them commit all manner of mayhem while I diligently take notes, bite my tongue, and go home to pick my nose."

"You're right. I agree there has to be a safety net. You see, that's why I need you. You know about kids."

When the waiter placed the chocolate cheese torte in front of John, Sydney knew there was no alternative but to wait again. He sipped his espresso as he watched his guest put fork to mouth. *I wonder if he can eat and think at the same time.*

Two minutes later, John pushed his empty plate aside. "You want my opinion, Syd?"

"I'm asking, John."

John had a dreamy look in his eyes. "I've never been quite sure about how to help the girls, but for the boys, I can envision an all-boys high school with a heavy emphasis on team sports."

Sydney blinked. *I don't think he's heard a word I said.*

"I think team sports build character, especially football. Get a young boy, a young sensitive boy like you were, put him on the football field, and he'll toughen up. He'll learn to defend himself."

Sydney winced. *Here we go again! Why is it that jocks seem to think football is the answer to all the problems facing adolescent boys?* He responded with a stone face. "I've never liked football. Tell me how you think my playing football could have changed the dynamics between us."

"First off, you wouldn't have been such a wimp—no offense." John offered the palms of his hands toward Sydney. "In football, guys learn to take care of themselves and, I might add, to take care of each other." John beamed as he enthusiastically slapped his palm on the table.

"I'm not sure I know what you mean," Sydney spoke in a monotone as he baited John. "To my mind, football is a brutal game. Kids are trained to fight with each other, not to get along with each other—"

"That's where you're wrong, Syd!" John's voice was loud; his stance, firm. "When you're part of a team, you have to depend on your teammates to be there for you, to protect you. You learn to get along with each other. Race, ethnicity, religion—none of it matters."

Sydney stared past John's shoulder toward the entrance where the headwaiter was talking to a group of prospective diners. *He sure is passionate about that game. You'd think he was defending his God.* He turned to John and asked, "What about the guys on the other team?"

"Same for them." John's voice sounded calm, but his face was flushed.

Sydney knew he was pushing John's buttons, but he couldn't seem to stop himself. Although he was equally passionate about his own stance, he kept his voice calm and in control. "They don't fight among themselves; they just fight with the guys on the other team. Doesn't that still mean that the guys on the winning team were better at fighting than the guys on the losing team? Isn't that teaching boys to win by using force—"

"It's not just about using force! There's strategy to it. You have to use your head, not just your brawn!"

Sydney's eyes narrowed as he snarled at John. "Is that why so many football players can't make it through college?"

John bounded to his feet and waved his arms in the air. "You're hitting pretty low here! We both know there's different kinds of smarts."

Sydney stood up and mocked John's arm-waving. "If you won't sit down and listen, I'll stand too. Let's get the whole damn restaurant in on it!"

The other diners stopped talking. The waiters stood rigidly fixed in place with their arms supporting trays suspended in the air. Sydney uttered an awkward apology, and the two men resumed their seats.

"Regardless of what kind of smarts we're talking about here, our brains should be used for getting along with each other, not beating each other up." Sydney cleared his throat, continuing despite John's grimace. "Cooperation is about the *fit*, not the fittest. Not the fittest, dammit. Listen to me, John!"

"Perhaps we ought to keep our voices down a little," John sniped back at Syd, making a show of looking around at the other diners. He put his hands in his lap with an exaggerated exhibition of civility. "Go on, Syd. I'm listening."

"What one has to offer is different from what the other has to offer. It can go up, or it can go down. It can work for us or against us. It's still us."

"You're not making any sense, Sydney."

"Football is about competition; it's not about cooperation!"

"But football's just a game, you see." John's voice sounded polite, but insincere.

"No, I don't see. It sounds like warfare to me."

"Warfare! You're taking it far too seriously, Syd. It's just a game—"

"You think I take it too seriously? Nobody takes it seriously enough, as far as I'm concerned." Sydney felt his heart throbbing as he pointed his finger at John. "A minute ago, you were trying to convince me that football was the answer to all the problems facing adolescent boys, and now you're saying it's just a game? Make up your mind, John. Which is it?"

"Calm down, Syd. You look like a man who's about to have a heart attack."

"Look, I'll spell it out for you. Everything you said about football applies to the military. Two armies are pitted against one another, and the mightiest one wins. There has to be teamwork; soldiers put their lives on the line, and they have to rely on their teammates to run interference. The team that kills and maims the most people gets the prize, the honors, and the medals."

John ran his fingers through his thinning gray hair. "Jeez, Syd. Nobody's supposed to get hurt in football— hold on now." He gave Syd the time-out signal. "I know you're going to jump all over that one. I admit people do get hurt, even paralyzed sometimes, but that's not the object."

"What *is* the object, John?"

"Winning…I guess the object is winning the game."

"Hah! When winning is the object and force is the means, I call that warfare!"

John cleared his throat. "But in football, boys are taught to play fair. There are rules."

Sydney snapped back, "There are rules in warfare, too."

"Nobody's expected to follow them. There's a big difference."

"When winning's important, people cheat."

"But it's not condoned."

"Get real, John. I've seen people cheering professional football; they get nuts. They cheer for the cheaters—if the cheaters are on the preferred team. High school's no different. Winning is more important than playing fair, and cheating *is* condoned. Admit it, John. Winning's more important than playing fair, just like in warfare!"

"You're getting loud again, Sydney. I'd hate for us to get kicked out of such a lovely restaurant."

Sydney lowered his voice to a normal pitch. "You want to put Susie on the football field? You want to train her to fight fair? Give me a break."

"That's the way the world is. There are winners and losers. And, yes, maybe we should let girls play the sport. I don't like it any more than you do, but I want my kids to be winners."

Sydney pointed his finger at John's nose. "Hah!"

"It's a tough, competitive world out there, Syd, or haven't you noticed? With all your money, I guess that's not an issue. These kids—my kids—they don't have rich daddies; they have to duke it out with the real world."

"Whose kids do you want to be losers, John?"

"That's not fair, Syd. I'm just talking reality here."

"The reality is that in competition, for every winner there has to be a loser." Sydney pushed for an answer. "Whose kids do you want to be losers?"

"The reality is that we live in a competitive society where there are winners and losers."

"The reality is that our very survival as a species depends on our ability to cooperate with each other. There's got to be a better way."

"Aren't you being a bit idealistic?"

"We should have evolved beyond the gladiator mentality, the Crusades mentality. Instead, we're destroying this grand and glorious Earth we are so fortunate to inhabit, and we're destroying ourselves. I fear for us, John." Sydney went on in a quiet voice. "If we continue to promote sports—games that mimic warfare, encourage violence, reward it, encourage cheating, and reward it, too—what will happen to us?"

John moaned. "I think you're being way too hard on football. I still think the sport builds character."

"Yeah, John, but what kind of character?"

"We can't change the world all by ourselves, Syd. Be realistic."

"OK, OK. I got a little carried away. We can't save the world all by ourselves. I agree—but maybe the young Susies and Jerrys can find a better way to get along with each other." Sydney's voice was respectful as he continued. "I wonder what would happen if we stopped pushing kids to compete with each other. Would they find a way to cooperate?"

John put his hands palms down on the table and looked Sydney in the eyes. "I'm not saying I agree with your thing about football, but you do give food for thought. We could do with some cooperation."

Sydney motioned to the waiter. "Bring us another bottle of Merlot. My friend and I have more business to conduct here. I'm glad you agree with me, John. Does that mean you're in?"

"I need more than this to go on. I can't say for sure, Syd."

Not in a mood to take no for an answer, Sydney pushed for action. "Why don't you start by finding out if we can use St. Joan's? You know about state standards for curriculum. You work on that piece. I want you to help interview and choose the staff. The teachers and the dorm chaperones will all have to agree to stay out of the way—"

"Except for obviously dangerous situations," John interjected.

Sydney smiled and nodded. "Except for obviously dangerous situations. I'll work on how to recruit the students and sell their families on it. And of course, I'll work on financing the whole thing. I'll have to sell some stock, and maybe a property or two. What do you say, John?"

"I don't know, Syd. You're expecting an awful lot from these kids."

"It's an experiment, John. Only a year, that's all I ask. What have we got to lose?"

"It would be a hard sell to the board, with a restriction on teaching religion and all, but the parish could use the rent money to do some maintenance and repair work. If the school will be empty on weekends, we could use it for our religious education classes then."

"How soon do you think you can get an answer from your board?"

"You're serious about this, Syd? You're really going to do this?"

"You're damned right I am. I'm going to do this, John—with you or without you."

"I'd have to get permission from the bishop. He pays my salary. He might have other plans for how I use my time."

"I feel it in my gut, John," Sydney implored. "You're the man for the job. I want you on board. Take a year's leave. I'll pay your salary. It's only a year."

"I just don't know, Syd."

Sensing that John was almost hooked, Sydney played his trump card. "Whatever happens after the year is over, I'll donate the money you need to reopen your school on your own terms."

"You'd do that? Syd? You'd do that?"

"Yes."

John took his handkerchief from his pocket, wiped his eyes, and blew his nose. "You drive a fair bargain, Syd—one I can't refuse. The bit about subsidizing St. Joan's School will go a long way toward selling it to the powers that be. Count me in."

The two men spent the next two hours strategizing and hammering out their separate tasks. They agreed on a time line, shook hands, and drank a toast to their partnership and their mission. "To the Schuster/Murphy project, an experimental school where we will learn from the children—the bullies and the victims."

Clink.

Chapter Four
Another Reunion
Early June 1996

"Park on the lot and wait for me, Kevin. I shouldn't be too long."

"It looks like it's locked, sir."

Sydney's eyes made a quick sweep of the questionable surroundings. "The street doesn't look like a very pleasant place to wait."

"Don't worry about me, sir. I'll be all right."

Sydney was on a mission. He knew he'd have to accept some risks. He glanced at the street one more time before he climbed the steps to the school entrance. Finding the door locked, he looked through the glass at the abandoned hall inside. He was about to leave when he noticed the buzzer.

After pressing the button, he peered through the window again. He punched the button a second time and glanced anxiously toward the limo. He checked his watch and rapped on the door.

He was about to give up when he saw Denise inside. She was running toward the door. She fiddled with the lock and shot him a wide-toothed smile. "Sydney, have you been out there long? I forgot the time. The buzzer doesn't always work. I know it's a nuisance, but you know how it is. Come in, come in."

"Hello, Denise. It's been a long time."

"Too long, Syd."

The two old friends stood facing one another, holding each other's hands.

"It's good to see you, Denise."

"You too, Syd."

"I know you're busy—end of school term and all. Thanks for squeezing me into your schedule—and for considering my plan."

"You sounded excited on the phone. I'm looking forward to hearing what you're up to. My office is down the hall. Shall we?" Denise led the way.

Once settled, Sydney declined her offer of a cup of coffee or a soft drink.

"You're looking well, Denise. The years have been kind to you."

Denise's smile was warm and friendly. "You're looking well yourself, Syd. Handsome as ever."

"Interesting neighborhood you have here—not exactly the kind of place where one feels free to leave doors open or expensive cars unattended."

"We do have the dubious distinction of having the highest number of violent drug-related crimes in the city. I've heard tell there's at least one violent death every weekend."

I should have told Kevin to drive off. I could still call him on the cell; have him come back and pick me up later, he thought. "I guess that explains the locked doors."

"It wasn't always like this. Polish immigrants originally settled the neighborhood. They were good, law-abiding citizens." Denise frowned. "Now, it's a volatile mix of every race, religion, and ethnic group you can imagine. It's virtually a war zone out there."

"Is it really that bad, Denise?"

"We've got everything from good, hard-working families with decent values to crack houses, prostitution, and drive-by shootings."

"Not my comfort zone. What keeps you here?"

"I make a good living. They pay principals well."

"Still, it sounds pretty discouraging."

"It is."

Sydney scrutinized Denise for a long time before he spoke. "Maybe—"

She interrupted. "On the phone, you said you had something important you wanted to talk to me about, Syd."

"Yes, I did. I've been giving a lot of thought to the dynamics between adolescent bullies and their victims. I'd like your opinion and, hopefully, your help."

"You said something about a plan…"

"Yes, an experiment that could shed some light on the subject. Five girls and five boys will be given an opportunity to receive half a million dollars each to pay their tuition and expenses at the college or technical school of their choice…. Do you mind if I take my jacket off?"

"Of course not."

"These ten children will attend classes together and live in a dormitory Monday through Friday. They'll go home during regular school holidays and on weekends. All of them must complete one year at the experimental school. If any one student leaves before the year is out, none of them will get the prize. There will, of course, be an exception for severe physical illness. If there are any drugs or alcohol on the school premises, all will lose. If any girl becomes pregnant, all will lose. Either they all win, or they all lose—together."

Sydney paused, leaned back in his chair, and folded his hands. "I think that pretty much covers it. You know, I think I would like a cola, Denise, if you don't mind. It's awfully warm in here."

"It's an old building—no air." She handed him a can from the tiny refrigerator on her credenza and gave him a plastic cup from her desk drawer. "Ice?"

"No, thank you. This is fine."

"You want to give a bunch of kids a lot of money to go to college, and all they have to do is keep their noses clean for a year. What's that supposed to prove?"

"Oops. I guess I left the most important piece out. Here's the catch, Denise. Students will be instructed not to seek adult intervention in their social relationships unless serious and immediate harm is threatened. If they can convince us at the end of the year that they've succeeded in solving—or really, evading—the bully/victim problem, and if they're able to describe to our satisfaction how they did it, I'll pay their way through college."

"How old are these kids?"

"Thirteen or fourteen—eighth grade."

"You're asking for trouble."

"I know."

"You want my advice?"

"Yes."

"I've been around kids that age for the past twenty-five years."

"That's why I'm asking you."

"I couldn't do it—I couldn't just sit by and let them get into all kinds of trouble. Here, with hundreds of them, it's easy to be apathetic. It's almost mandatory. But with ten in an intimate setting..." Denise shook her head. "I just couldn't do it."

That's what John said, Sydney thought. "If the adults intervene, the children won't have the opportunity to work things out for themselves. We'd have a school like any other. What could we learn from that?"

Sydney took Denise's silence as an invitation to go on. "All adult personnel at the school will be carefully instructed not to meddle in the affairs of the students unless they perceive a seriously dangerous situation. Meddling on their part could potentially rob the children of their prize."

"I hope you're using the word 'affairs' broadly here. Do you intend to hand out condoms?"

"I hadn't considered that issue yet, but I'm sure the local pharmacy sells them."

"I'm not kidding, Syd."

"Neither am I."

"You know, Syd, kids aren't all proficient in the same ways. Some are book-smart. For others, college wouldn't be an appropriate incentive."

"We'll cross that bridge when we come to it."

Denise quizzed Sydney about his theories of aggression and submission, listening with apparent interest. But when he expounded on his thoughts about football, she cut him off.

"Oh? So contact sports are the culprit for our violent teens, huh?" she said. "I guess that means the media, parents, drugs, poverty, and a hundred other things I could mention have been let off the hook?"

Why doesn't anybody seem to understand how insidiously harmful the game is? "OK, OK, we can't blame everything on football." Sydney pursed his lips.

Denise looked at him as though he'd lost his sanity. "What's with this sudden interest in the youth of America, Sydney? Since when did you think you had something to learn from a bunch of pimply-faced adolescents?"

Sydney let his face soften. His tone was gentle. "You sound bitter."

"Just burnt out," she sighed. "If you want to do something important, why not just skip all the games and give scholarships to disadvantaged kids who show promise? I could supply you with the names of an endless stream of good kids who will never get a chance." She looked at him with imploring eyes.

"It's something I have to do, Denise—and you're wrong. I think we do have something to learn from the kids. This thing, this experiment, could give us some crucial insights into ways to stop minor bullying from escalating into major violence. You've got to admit we have a problem with that."

"Oh, there's a problem, all right." Denise opened a drawer, reached in and dumped several weighty-looking documents on her desk. "And all the locked doors, metal detectors, locker searches, increased surveillance, zero tolerance, teach tolerance, psychotherapy, punishments, drug education, sex education, peer mediation, and pleading with the kids to seek help from authorities who are too burnt out to give a damn isn't making a dent."

Sydney carefully contemplated the scowl on Denise's face for a moment before he spoke again. "Back when we were in college, I was the bitter one. You were always upbeat, the fun one, the optimist. I guess that's what attracted me to you—what made me fall in love with you."

He was pleased that he was still able to make her blush.

Denise took a can of cola from the refrigerator and poured herself a cup. "I still don't understand why the sudden interest. You could be taking your grandchildren to Paris Disney."

"Why is that important, Denise? Why do you need to know my motive?"

"Come on, Syd. I thought we were friends. We had a special bond once; I know we haven't stayed in contact, but I've always thought that we had the kind of friendship where we could just pick it up where we left off. We used to be able to talk things out."

I wonder where fate would have taken us, Denise—if you hadn't jilted me for Fred. "Look, I'll tell you and Fred all about it at dinner sometime. Right now, I just want your help with the experiment."

"Fred died three years ago, Sydney. Cancer got him."

"You didn't tell me; I'm sorry to hear that."

"No. Well. It's a long story."

A tender smile spread slowly across Sydney's face as the image of a younger version of Denise flashed through his mind. He had feelings that he thought he'd buried along with his irretrievable youth.

"I'll be in town for the weekend; some business in Menomonee Falls. Let's have dinner on Saturday and self-disclose. I guess that's the word—you show me yours, and I'll show you mine…"

Denise had a twinkle in her eye. "I have a date with my laundry, but I think I can beg off."

She still has that same old flirtatious way about her. He hesitated for a moment before he said, "Right now, I'd like to get back to the project, if you don't mind?"

Denise nodded her agreement.

"You've got some of the basics. I thought maybe we could select the students from your school. Maybe you could help me sell the parents on the idea."

Denise nearly spilled her soft drink. "Are you sure you want your students to come from *this* school, Sydney? Why not choose some nice, all-white suburban school? They've got the same problems, and those kids speak your language. Are you deliberately trying to make it hard on yourself?"

"It looks to me like the kids from this neighborhood are dealing with some very real problems—serious ones, not the kind of problems people make up in their heads. The differences between them are greater, more visible. They act; they don't just talk, intellectualize, and rationalize. Behavior is easier to see and to learn from."

"Oh, these kids act, all right. They talk, too—I just wonder if you'd be able to understand their language."

Sydney loosened his tie and opened the top button on his shirt. "Besides, the prize might not be enough of an incentive for suburban kids who will probably go to college anyway."

"What about activities outside of school?"

"They'll be on their own."

When Sydney caught the baffled look on Denise's face, he added, "The streets in Menomonee Falls—that's where the school is—are safer than where they currently spend their time."

"I'm not saying that I'm agreeing to have the students come from my school, but what would be your criteria for selecting them?"

"No criteria. I'm not a social scientist, but I think it would be helpful if they knew one another—maybe already had some sort of relationship going. But I'd like it to be kind of a random selection too, like maybe a lottery."

"You're right about one thing, Syd. You're not a social scientist."

"No, I'm not. I have the same burning questions, but I'm not restricted by bureaucratic conventions."

"You could end up with some real troublemakers."

"Yes, I know, but that's the plan. I expect there'll be some smart alecks. There'll be some pushovers, too. That's the beauty of it. Can the aggressive ones and the meek ones find a way to peacefully coexist?"

"It could as easily turn nasty too, you know."

"I'm aware there's that risk. If it turns out nasty, we can learn from that too."

"I don't know you anymore, Sydney Schuster. When did you become such a risk taker? You used to be so cautious; I might even say a wimp."

Sydney winced. *Was it so obvious to everybody but me?* "I think you'd agree we're not doing so well by them with the current system. What the hell, Denise—what have we got to lose?"

"Only a couple of lives, I guess. These kids can get pretty violent, and some of them play for keeps."

"Denise, look around you." Sydney gestured toward the window. "We're already losing them—at least one violent crime every weekend."

"What happens to them after you've finished with them?"

"They go back to business as usual."

Denise stared out the window. "Never mind the screwed-up family dynamics, the drugs, and the culture of street violence." She turned to look at Sydney and pointed her finger at him. "Most of these kids won't make it to college with the kind of academic preparation they'll get in high school after your little experiment is over. You can't just pluck them up, promise them a better way, and drop them back where you left them!"

Sydney blinked. "Thank you, Denise. I never thought of that aspect. I see your point. If they win the grand prize, at least some are going to need a leg up. You're right."

Sydney thought for a moment before he offered his solution. "Let's say they get the $500,000 upon completion of the project instead of when they enter college. The money goes in the bank. They can't touch the principal until they begin college, but the interest could be used for any remedial work or private schooling they'd need."

"Well, that would help, but it would still be hard to sell the parents on the idea."

"Oh, come on, Denise—you've got to be kidding. I'm offering these kids a chance at life. What kind of parent could possibly say no?"

"It's one thing for kids to live in a dangerous environment by default, but what you're suggesting is dangerous *by design*—you don't seem to understand that, but their parents might. And I still want to know what happens to them if they fail."

"If they fail, we'll have learned something. Hopefully, we'll have learned something useful." Sydney took a deep breath. "Perhaps we'll have to accept that which we cannot change. But even that would be of some solace." *At least to me.*

"You're going to do this, Syd. Even before you came here, you'd already decided."

"Yes, Denise, I'm going to do it. John Murphy's on board. I'd like you there too. But you're right—I'm going to do this, no matter what."

"John Murphy? That name sounds familiar. Wasn't he…"

"Yes, he's the one."

"Now I'm really curious."

"Will you help me, Denise?"

"You sound like a man in a hurry."

"I'm not getting any younger."

"School's out for the summer. How would we do a lottery with no students present to pull the numbers from the hat?"

"I don't know; maybe you should pick them." Sydney looked at his watch. "Damn, I forgot all about Kevin. He must be cooked by now. I pay him well, but not that well. What do you say, Denise? Will you help me?"

"I'll think about it, Syd."

"Look, I gotta go. Kevin waiting in a limo with the windows up and the doors locked for two hours is not a pretty picture."

Denise got up and headed for the door. Sydney put his right hand out, palm toward her. "That's all right, Denise, I can find my way."

"I'll have to lock after you."

"Oh, that's right…I forgot."

Sydney gave Denise a friendly hug at the door. "I'll call you about Saturday. We'll catch up more then."

He hurried out of the building to the limo and let himself into the front passenger seat. "I'm so sorry, Kevin. Where was my head? I should have told you to take a break, drive down to the lake, grab lunch, visit a museum, something. Anything! I see you've at least opened the windows."

"I realized I could die from asphyxiation or a bullet, sir. Since a bullet is quicker, I opened the windows."

"Start the motor. Get some air in here. God, it's hot." Sydney wiped his brow with his handkerchief. "I have to admit, I took a certain comfort in knowing you'd be here waiting. I didn't want to be alone in this neighborhood. I should be paying you for being a bodyguard. Oh, I'm rambling. All I can say is that I'm sincerely sorry."

"It was a bit of a scare, sir, and a long wait. I tried to read this book you gave me about the value of cooperation, but in this environment, I found it a little hard to get into. I was thinking about what I'd do if the gang of boys who circled the car made a move to take it. I decided I'd cooperate and just let them have it."

"That would have been a wise choice, Kevin."

"As it turned out, I had a lively discussion with them. They had a lot of questions. They left peaceably enough. How did your meeting with Ms. Hanover go? Do you think she'll help with the project?"

"She thinks I'm a little crazy, but I have a hunch she's going to help."

The conversation trailed off as they negotiated their way back to the highway. Sydney couldn't hold back a satisfied smile, and he didn't mind when Kevin noticed.

"Do you plan to see her again, sir?"

"Again and again, I hope."

Chapter Five
Dinner and Self-Disclosure
Early June 1996

Sydney noticed a slight shift in the window curtain as the limo arrived in front of Denise's house, but he had to ring the bell twice before she answered.

"Hello, Sydney." Her smile was warm and inviting. "You're a little early."

He took Denise's hand in both of his while his eyes scanned the room. "Hi, Denise. Nice place you have here."

"Thank you. I like it. Would you like a drink or something before we go?"

"That would be nice. Thank you."

"I have scotch and brandy. I don't care much for brandy myself, but no self-respecting Wisconsin native would fail to offer her guest brandy. What am I saying? You know that. You're from the Midwest."

"Scotch and water would be fine."

As Sydney made himself comfortable in the front room, Denise disappeared into the kitchen. She returned momentarily with their drinks.

Sidney tasted his drink. "Hmmm. This is fine."

Denise put a couple of napkins on the coffee table and sat in the chair across from Sydney.

Sydney took another sip. "If I'd have known it was single malt, I would have had it straight up."

"I can get you another." Denise leaned toward Sydney and reached for his glass.

"No, this is fine; sit down, I didn't know Milwaukee had such a nice neighborhood. It's like a little Camelot here."

"The Milwaukee Public School System requires its employees to live in the city. If you have to live in Milwaukee, Washington Highlands is the place to be—unless you can afford Lake Drive, that is. And the best part for me is that I'm not likely to encounter my students on my own time and on my own safe little turf."

"Last time I saw you—what was it, twenty years ago?—you couldn't wait to roll up your sleeves and help all those disadvantaged kids in the inner city."

"I was idealistic, wasn't I? And naïve."

"Is it the drugs? The drugs and the violence that hardened you, made you apathetic?" Sydney's voice was compassionate.

"I suppose…but more than that, it was how the relationship between the kids and me changed."

"As I recall, you always got along well with adolescents—even the tough, smart-alecky ones."

"I thought so, too." Denise raised her eyebrows. "Until one night about five years ago, when three seventh-grade boys wearing masks attacked me in the parking lot. They demanded my purse; they pushed me down. One of them hit me in the face.... How could they be so stupid? How could they even think I wouldn't recognize them?" She shook two fists at the air. "I was their teacher!"

"Did you press charges?"

"Yes, but that's beside the point. It wasn't the violence I minded so much, or even their stupidity. I cared about those boys. I thought they cared about me as a human being. No, it wasn't the violence; it was the betrayal. They violated a sacred trust bond."

"You gave them your heart and your trust, and they beat you up and took your purse. Only a martyr would be foolish enough to be that vulnerable again." Sydney finished his drink. In a kind and gentle voice, he said, "So, what's next? What's next for you, Denise?"

"In a couple more years, I'll retire. I'd like to do some traveling. There's always something new to look forward to, don't you think?"

"I guess." Sydney stood up and looked at his watch. "We'd better get started. I thought we'd go to Scottie's Crab House."

"Scottie's Crab House? How did you find out about Scottie's? It's the best-kept secret in Milwaukee! Fabulous choice, Syd."

Sydney took Denise's arm and escorted her to the limo.

Denise nodded toward Kevin and winked at Sydney. "He's cute. Are we taking him with us?"

"No, not this time. Kevin will drop us off and pick us up later. I'll call him on the cell and tell him when we're ready to leave."

Denise nestled herself into the back seat. "You're in for a real treat, Syd. The chef at Scottie's works some kind of magic."

"The waiter I talked with when I made the reservations told me there's a nice little alcove on the second floor, in a corner by itself—a perfect place where people can talk in private. I've reserved it for us." Sydney was talking as he got in beside her.

"I know the room you're talking about. It's cozy, but I'm shocked that you could reserve it. Scottie's doesn't take reservations."

"A generous tip can be very persuasive."

When they pulled up to the restaurant, Sydney looked out the window. "This is it? This is Scottie's? It looks like somebody's house." He got out and offered Denise his hand.

"Yes, this is Scottie's," she said. "It might not look like much on the outside, but it's a lot more than the somebody's house it used to be."

Kevin waved. "Have a pleasant evening, sir. I'll wait for your call."

After they were seated, Denise peeked at the menu while the waiter poured water. "Kevin seems like a nice guy."

"He is."

"How long's he been with you?"

"Let me think a minute. Ten—no, eleven years. What'll you have to drink? I'm in the mood for wine."

"Sounds good to me. You order. What I don't know about wine would fill volumes."

Sydney ordered a bottle of Chablis. After he and Denise had placed their food orders, Sydney gave Denise his full attention as he moved the conversation to a more intimate level.

"So, tell me, Denise, what about you?"

"There's not a whole lot to tell, Syd. By your standards, I probably live a pretty dull life. After the chicks flew the nest, there wasn't much left for Fred and me to do— together, I mean."

"You and Fred split up? Wish I'd known sooner. I would have been there for you." *I could have been there with you,* he thought.

"Maybe all those years of teaching at MPS had made me too dull for him. It's the typical run-of-the-mill story. Successful businessman seeks excitement and ends up with trophy wife and new kid."

"That must have been very difficult for you, Denise. You should have let me know."

"Too busy fighting, I guess. Old wife fights new wife for loyalty of children and grandchildren. Old wife wins some battles and loses some."

The waiter arrived with their wine, and Sydney did the usual tasting routine. "This will be fine." The waiter poured more wine for Sydney, filled Denise's glass, and disappeared. They each took a few sips of the wine. Denise nodded her approval, and Sydney, anxious to know more about Denise's past—where he might stand with her, now that Fred was out of the picture—picked up the converstation where they'd left off. "You said Fred died from cancer?"

"Yeah, he got cancer and the sympathy of the kids, who suddenly became very attentive and cozy with him and the Trophy."

"And what about you? How'd you handle all that?"

"All's well that ends well, I guess. Trophy wife got her just reward. She ended up nursing Fred and entertaining his family for seven years. The money was used up on medical expenses and heroic procedures to prolong his useless life. Now she's too old to be somebody else's trophy wife, and she's got a ten year-old kid to raise. Tsk, tsk. Guess she'll just have to fend for herself."

Sydney reached for his wine and responded warmly, "Sounds like you've been to hell and back."

"Yeah, well, that's history." Denise took a deep breath and went on. "Things are better now. My children have married nice people, and my grandchildren are doing well. Two are freshmen in high school, and the other two are in middle school. Thank God they live in the suburbs. Say what you will about the sorry state of our schools, Waukesha is still a pretty good place to raise a family. Why don't you do your lottery thing in Waukesha?"

"Would you want your grandchildren to attend my school?"

"I'll be honest with you, Syd. I think your idea is a little crazy."

"Maybe…"

The waiter placed their entrées on the table and freshened their water. "Will there be anything else?"

"No, thank you. This looks fine." Sydney raised his glass to make a toast. "Here's to finding a relationship that shouldn't have gotten lost."

Denise and Sydney engaged in small talk and savored their scrumptious Cajun dinner in the privacy of the alcove. When they'd finished the main course, the waiter cleared the table and brought the dessert menu.

"This looks wonderful, but I don't think I could eat another bite." Denise handed her menu back to the waiter.

"We'll just work on this for a while if you don't mind." Sydney pointed to the half-full bottle of wine. The waiter refilled their glasses and disappeared.

Denise sipped her wine. "OK, your turn. Remember, you promised. Tell me why you're so hell-bent on doing this experiment."

"For myself, I guess." Sydney pushed his glass aside. "It's too late for Simon and Ruben. Maybe it's for my grandkids too. I don't know."

"Tell me about Simon and Ruben. Last time I saw them was at Shirley's funeral. They were nice little rascals."

"They've grown up to be ugly big rascals. I failed them, Denise. God knows I tried, but I failed them."

"C'mon, Syd. I have a hard time believing you were anything but a kind and caring father."

"Look, Denise, I'm going to tell you about Simon and Ruben because I promised I would. It's not something I like to think about, so I'm going to get through it as quickly as I can."

"You don't have to tell me, Syd, if you don't want to."

"You'll just wheedle it out of me later anyway. Might as well get it over with."

Sydney cleared his throat. "In high school, Ruben played varsity football—could have gotten scholarships to the best universities. Not that he needed them; he could have gone anywhere he chose. He chose to go to prison."

Tears welled up in Sydney's eyes as he struggled to talk past the lump in his throat. "He killed his wife, Denise. Thank God there were no children."

"Oh, Syd. I'm so sorry."

"It was a long time ago, but things like that…" He shook his head. "Ruben and the girl were just kids themselves when they got married. It all happened so fast." Sydney felt his voice shaking.

Denise put her hand on Sydney's wrist. "What happened, Syd—what happened so fast?"

Sydney took his handkerchief from his pocket, brushed at his eyes, and blew his nose. "Ruben liked to get his way. He treated people like he owned them, like their sole purpose in life was to make Ruben happy. People crossed Ruben at their own peril."

Sydney's voice sounded distant to him, like someone else was talking and he was just mouthing the words. "When a dealer hit on his wife, Ruben went into a jealous rage. Accused her of asking for it, of flirting with the dealer. She denied it. There was a big scene in the casino. They left together while Ruben was still raging at her." Sydney looked straight at Denise and whispered, "He killed her with his bare hands, Denise. Beat her to a bloody pulp and strangled her in their hotel room." Sydney closed his eyes and swayed back and forth.

Denise reached across the table and rubbed Sydney's arm. "I don't know what to say. What Ruben did, what Ruben became—it's not your fault."

"Look, Denise, I'm feeling a little ill. Excuse me for a few minutes, will you? I need some air."

"I'll go with you." Denise was halfway out of her chair.

"No, no. Please. You stay here."

Sydney headed for the men's room. The wrenching in his stomach wouldn't let up. *I was afraid this would happen,* he thought as he stood over the urinal and heaved. *I got through Ruben. Simon will be a little easier.* He cupped his hands to catch some water from the faucet, rinsed his mouth, washed his hands, and headed back to the table.

"Sorry, Denise." He sat down and took a drink of his water. "You've only heard the half of it. I have another son, you know. For better or for worse, at least he's not in jail—yet."

The waiter approached the table, and Denise waved him away. "After what you told me about Ruben, I was afraid to ask about Simon. You don't have to do this, Syd. You don't have to tell me if you don't feel up to it."

"No, it's OK. I've gone this far; I'm going to be finished with it."

"Only if you want to—"

"I wouldn't bail Simon out of a jam when he was kicked out of the university. So he went into the waste management business with Shirley's brother, Frankie

Sardino. I think he did it to spite me. He knew what I thought of Sardino."

"Sardino…yes, I think I've heard the name."

"Simon's a glorified garbage man. I know his dealings include a lot more than just picking up people's trash. My guess is he's selling people trash—trash and protection. It's been ten years since we've had words. Simon wants me to use whatever power or money I can to get Ruben out of prison, but I just can't do it. Ruben's my son, Denise, but sometimes I think the death penalty would have been better. At least it would be over."

Sydney took a deep breath, and his voice got a little stronger. "My therapist told me that my anger was more healthy than my sadness and self-recrimination. I vowed that neither of my sons—not Simon, not Ruben—would get one more dime of my money. They'd just use it to push people around, and I won't have that!"

Denise took hold of Sydney's hand. "I don't have words, Syd."

"It's all right, Denise. It was a very long time ago. Sometimes it seems like something that happened to someone else." Sydney quietly stared out the window at nothing in particular.

Denise broke the silence. "You mentioned grandchildren?"

"Two boys, eleven and thirteen. I haven't seen them since they were babies. I don't expect they'll become the kind of men I'd want to know—being raised by Simon and all. But then, what do I know? If the proof were in the pudding, I sure wouldn't get any merit badges for being a good father. And there you have it, Denise—my motive. I guess I'd like a better shot for my grandsons. Not just them—all the kids."

"A lesser man wouldn't bother." She reached for his hand.

"Well, then there's the John Murphy piece. I haven't told you about my friend, John Murphy. Father John Murphy, that is."

"You do mean the same John Murphy—the one who beat you up and gave you nightmares?"

"Yes, I do."

"This I gotta hear."

"I feel better now that all that self-disclosure stuff is out of the way. Believe it or not, I'm a little hungry. How about some dessert?"

"Scottie makes a wonderful chocolate mousse."

Sydney poked his head around the corner and signaled to the waiter. "Two orders of chocolate mousse, please."

Over dessert, Sydney filled Denise in on how he and John came to peace with each other, and he asked if she'd given the idea of helping with the project any further thought.

Denise reached into her purse and took out a neatly folded piece of paper. "Actually, I've done a bit more than just think about it." She unfolded the paper. "You wanted five boys and five girls—preferably boys and girls who know each other, randomly selected. You do realize, Sydney, that that's almost a contradiction in terms. I randomly selected one class of students, and from that class, I randomly selected ten students." She smiled as she handed him the paper.

Sydney read the names out loud. "Robert Austin. Karter Johnson. Eduardo Cortez. Mohandas Shastri. Sam Smith. Jenna Stein. Melissa Whistler. Tashina Jones. Theresa Winter. Maria Guliano. Sounds like a good mix." Sydney smiled. "Hello, my young friends, we're about to have an adventure."

"I know these kids. I seriously considered cheating, hand-selecting a different bunch. I still could—"

"No, I wouldn't want you to do that. And no, I don't want to consider a different school."

She took the list from Sydney's hand and read the names. "Robert Austin; can't figure him out, too good to be true. My guess—he's a little fake, just waiting to get out from under his father's thumb so he can become the little delinquent he was genetically programmed to be.

"Karter Johnson; he's a real winner!" she sneered. "All hormones—well, not *all* hormones. The combination is dangerous. It's not that Karter doesn't have brains, but at this stage of his life, Karter uses his brains to satisfy his hormones.

"Eduardo Cortez; he and Karter together? Give me a break. Don't even want to think about it. Eddie's not as smart as Karter is; he's easily influenced. Eddie will do Karter's bidding.

"Sydney, do you have any idea what you're doing here?"

"Go on."

"Mohandas Shastri; Moe's a nice kid; they'll chew him up and spit out the pieces.

"Then there's Sam Smith; he's a real charmer. Nice-looking boy; he's got a smile that would vaporize dry ice in thirty seconds flat. Sam always seems to be in a good mood. I wonder about his dark side. Everybody has one."

"Aren't you being a little cynical?"

"If I could, I'd talk you out of this, Syd."

"You can't."

"I know."

"What about the girls?"

"Melissa Whistler; Melissa the mouse. Mousy Melissa, darting here, darting there, hiding from the cats. Melissa could use a rescue. She'd have to find a different survival strategy, though. It'll be hard for her to be invisible in a school with only nine other kids.

"Tashina Jones; now there's a cat who can take care of herself. No need to worry about her.

"Theresa Winter; her mother will never let her go.

"Jenna Stein; Jenna and her twin transferred here from another school recently." Denise had a far-off look, and her voice got suddenly quiet. "They're academically way ahead of the rest…"

She sounded more like she was in possession of her voice again as she continued. "And rounding things out nicely, Sydney, we have Maria Guliano. You said you wanted smart alecks and pushovers. You've got your little pushover here. Karter and Eddie will be up to no good with her. That's for sure."

"Thanks, Denise. I mean it." Sydney wasn't sure his heart was pounding because his plan was becoming a reality or because Denise was going to be a part of it. "I guess the next thing to do is to arrange a meeting with the kids and their parents."

"When do you want to do that?"

"The sooner the better."

Sydney motioned to the waiter for more coffee. "Now the teachers, that's a different story. I do want them hand-picked. Any thoughts on that?"

"I'll think about it. I know my way around the system, and I think I have a pretty good idea about what kind of teachers you're looking for."

"John will need to be in on the final selection, though. He'll be the one working very closely with them. And thank you, Denise. This means a great deal to me." He took the cell phone from his pocket and punched in a few numbers. "Kevin, we're ready to leave now." He looked up at Denise. "He'll be here in a few minutes. Waiter, check please."

In the car, Sydney told Denise that he'd be flying to Los Angeles on business the next day. "I'll give you a call toward the end of the week. If you're free, we can do dinner again. Now that the self-disclosure stuff is out of the way, it should be a more pleasant evening."

Chapter Six
Selection and Application
Early July 1996

John, who was sitting on the edge of Denise's desk, gestured for Jake Stein to sit down. "We'd like to get some background information about your daughter, Mr. Stein."

Jake remained standing. "What's this all about? As an attorney, I'd like to know what's going on with my daughter before I say anything else."

"My apologies, Mr. Stein." John's face flushed. "I forgot. You don't know why we asked you here. Mr. Schuster, Ms. Hanover, and I have talked about the plan so much among ourselves, I guess I went too fast. Please do have a seat."

Jake sat in one of the six chairs that had been arranged in a circle for the purpose of the interviews. Sydney explained the experimental school and the prize to him.

Jake ran his fingers through his hair and took a deep breath. "That could be quite an opportunity for Jenna, especially under the circumstances. What would you like to know?"

John pulled his chair closer to Jake's. "First, we'd asked that both parents attend this meeting. Is there some reason why the girl's mother isn't here?"

"Jenna's mother and I have been divorced for some time. I have sole custody of Jenna, her twin sister, and their younger brother."

"They live with you, then?"

"With me, my wife, and our two little ones."

"Five children? That's quite a houseful."

"Tell me about it, Father—you're a priest, aren't you? I noticed the collar. So this experimental school thing, it's not a Catholic school, is it?"

John cleared his throat. "No, it's not. The students will be free to practice whatever religion they're comfortable with."

"It sounds a little risky, having ten children in each other's company twenty-four hours a day with no adult supervision, don't you think?"

"They're to solve their own social problems, Mr. Stein. That doesn't mean they'll be completely unsupervised. There'll be teachers and house parents on the premises at all times. I myself will be keeping a close watch. If there are signs of real danger, one of us is bound to pick it up." John made a note to talk to Sydney about covering that base more thoroughly in the next presentations. "Do you have any other questions?"

"No. Not yet."

"I have one," Denise interjected. "Mr. Stein, can you see any reason why your daughter shouldn't participate in this experiment?"

"No, no. I think this could turn out to be a good chance for her. God knows I can't afford to give her the kind of education she's been led to expect."

Denise called Jenna into the office and explained the plan to her. "Do you understand, Jenna? Do you have any questions?"

The girl stared straight ahead. "I won't go without Becca."

Jake put one knee on the floor by Jenna's chair and took her hand. "Don't be hasty, Jenna. You need to think about this. We need to talk about it. Becca should have a say in it too."

"I'm not going without Becca, Dad. That's just how it is. There's nothing to talk about."

"I'll talk to her and get back to you," Jake said as he and Jenna left the office.

Denise poured herself a glass of water and sat back in the chair behind her desk. "I'm sorry, guys. I should have warned you about Jenna's mother. It's such a sad story. She almost died of asphyxiation. The twins were the ones to find her in the garage. That was about six months ago."

"Tragedy. I suppose that could explain Jenna's reluctance to leave her sister. Do you think she'll change her mind—about the school, I mean?" John fingered through his notes.

*****

Raymond Austin, Robert's father, was the next to be interviewed. After politely listening to the plan, Raymond barked, "You people must think I'm crazy! I run a tight ship at my house. Robert does exactly what I tell him. I'm not about to send him off to some cockamamie experiment where things are run by a bunch of kids. If other parents want their kids to be guinea pigs, that's up to them, but not my kid. No way!"

Raymond stormed out of the office and roared across the large waiting area to his son. "Come on, Robert. We'll go home now."

Denise had an a-ha grin on her face. "That explains why Robert seems like such an uptight little fake. He wouldn't dare get caught doing anything that wasn't strictly according to the books with that guy for a father."

*****

John was going over some papers with a secretary in the outer office when he noticed the Smiths. They were sitting behind the counter that separated the two parts of the room. John discreetly watched and listened.

Chapter Six

George looked at his watch. "We're early. So what do you think, Samantha? What did the woman on the phone say to you again?"

"Something like, 'Your son Sam has been chosen by a process of random selection to participate in a scientific experiment designed to discover how cooperation could impact the problem of bullying in our schools.' She sounded like a robot. Then she said something about a college scholarship. It was strange. She stopped right in the middle of her sentence and said, 'You'll need to hold your questions for the interview, Mrs. Smith.' I guess she wasn't supposed to say anything about the scholarship."

"Sure got my attention. You know Sam can be a bit of a bully sometimes." He looked at his son. "You know you can, Sam."

"Just because I get a little rough with Marty," the boy whined. "You don't see it. You don't see the whole thing. That kid can be a real pain in the royal behind. He bugs me."

Samantha put her finger on her lips. "Shhh."

"All I have to do is look at him sideways, and he goes running to Mom. He's the one with the problem, not me!"

"Sam, I said, 'shhh.'"

"Is this going to be some kind of therapy for bullies or something?"

George's voice was soft but firm. "I don't know, son. Whatever it is, it might be a chance for you to get a college scholarship. It's an experiment; that means it has a beginning and an end. Experiments don't last forever. I

The Prize

suggest you be open to a little inconvenience for that kind of reward. Think how it could change your life, son."

"Your dad and I didn't have it so easy, you know." Samantha pointed her finger at the boy. "No scholarships and no family money for us. We had to work our butts off, and we're still paying off the student loans."

George picked up where Samantha left off. "We've got some set aside for you, and we'll help all we can, but we're not rich. You'd have to go to a state college, and you'd still have to work part time. Paying some dues now could make it a lot easier for you later."

John cleared this throat. "Excuse me, I'm Father John Murphy. I couldn't help overhearing your conversation. If you'd like to join us inside, my colleagues and I will explain the whole thing." He turned to the boy and said, "Sam, you'll have to wait a bit longer. We'd like to talk with your parents first."

John led the way past a row of vacant desks, tidy and undisturbed for the summer break.

George and Samantha listened carefully to Sydney's explanation. "I'm a social studies teacher," George enthusiastically responded. "I can absolutely relate. This is a fascinating way to address an important social problem. Wish I'd have thought of it. Do you need any teachers?"

"That base is not quite covered yet." John shook his head and looked to Sydney for an explanation.

Sydney smiled at George. "I'm sure you are a fine teacher, Mr. Smith. You'd probably be a good addition to the staff. However, given the nature of the experiment, it wouldn't do for a father and son to be involved in it together. I hope you understand. All parents will be informed about the qualifications of the teachers as soon as we have signed contracts."

When Sam was filled in, his face lit up. "I can't think of anything better than not putting up with Marty all the time. Will kids really be allowed to work things out for themselves?" He looked at John for his answer.

"That's the idea."

"Who else is going to be there?"

"I am—I'll be your principal."

"Is this going to be a Catholic school?"

"No. The school is upstairs from a church, though."

John quickly glanced at Sydney before asking, "Are you Catholic?"

"No. We don't go to church. Am I supposed to call you Father?"

John smiled at the boy. "Don't worry, son. You'll get used to it."

*****

At the end of their interview, Shanita Jones and her daughter Tashina clapped their hands and gave each other high-fives.

Tashina went straight to Maria's house to tell her the good news.

Maria put six plates on the table, dished up the salad, and stirred the marinara sauce on the stove. "The mostaccioli is almost done. Do you want to eat with us, Tashina?"

"You do all dat by yourself?"

Maria's mother bounded into the kitchen, grabbed an apron, and washed her hands in the kitchen sink. "Call Terry and Tony," she said to Maria. "Hi, Tashina. You staying to eat with us?"

"I jus come over to tell Maria bout me gettin to go to a different school next year—and maybe gettin a lotta money so I can go to college. Can you see it? Me! Me, lil ol Tashina Jones goin to college!"

Maria set an extra plate for Tashina. "I got picked too," she said in a monotone.

"Nah—don't mess wit me, girl. You got picked?"

"Yeah."

Tashina poked Maria's shoulder and skipped around the table. "You and me, Maria, we goin together! Come on, girl, kick them heels."

Maria ignored Tashina's enthusiasm as she continued to go about the business of getting supper on the table.

Tashina stopped her skipping and gawked at Maria. "What's a matter? You don't look too happy."

"I said I got picked. I didn't say I was going."

Dinner was a hubbub of activity with the noise of forks scraping on plates, the passing of food, and everyone talking with mouths full. Terry raised her hand to get her mother's attention. "Ma, does this mean that Maria won't be living with us anymore?"

"She'll be home on the weekends. It's gonna be tough around here without Maria to help out," Connie moaned. "I guess you and your brother are going to have to learn to cook and do dishes."

Terry and Tony responded in unison. "Aw, Ma!"

Richie reached across the table for some more pasta. "They're just kids, Connie."

"It's a cinch that you're not going to pick up the slack, Richie."

"Get off it, Connie."

"The 'kids' are ten and eleven years old, for God's sake. Maria's been doing it since she was nine. It might be good for them to take on a little responsibility."

Maria started to clear the table. "Mom, I'm not so sure I can do this."

Tashina picked up a couple of plates and carried them to the sink. "What you sayin, girl? Course you can do it!"

"Your father and I have already decided, Maria. You'll do fine, sweetie—if you just put your mind to it."

Connie pushed her chair back from the table and wiped her hands on her apron. "OK, come on, Terry. You too, Tony. You might as well get used to it. You're about to learn a valuable lesson in life. I'll show you how to clear the table and do the dishes. Tomorrow, we'll work on laundry."

Tony's eyes got big and wide. "Ma, guys don't do dishes—tell her, Dad."

Connie shot Richie a look that said, "You'd better keep your mouth shut if you know what's good for you."

"Do what your mother says, Tony."

Tony gave Maria his meanest scowl and then looked straight at his mother. "What about Rick?"

Connie handed a plate to Tony. "Take this to the sink and rinse it. I'll show you how to load the dishwasher." She glared at Richie. "Ask your father about Rick. Your father's the one that got him that car. At sixteen, Rick thinks he's a man already. He doesn't have to do chores. Like father, like son."

Connie picked up some silverware and handed it to Terry. "Go! Go, Maria. Sit down and talk to your friend. You're not doing dishes tonight." She gave Maria a gentle shove.

Maria and Tashina went upstairs to the bedroom Maria shared with her sister and closed the door.

"I don't get you, Maria. Why you so gloomy?" Tashina sat cross-legged on the bed. "Thought you hated dat stupid school much as me."

"I do hate it as much as you do—maybe more! But at least I get to come home at night. I don't have to stay there *all* the time."

"Yeah, you gets to come home, all right. You gets to come home and take care a them. What's dat?"

Maria sighed. "Who else do you think will be there—in the school?"

"They ain't lettin out wit dat information, girl. They's keepin it a top secret."

"It's bad enough trying to stay out of the way when guys hassle me all day. I don't want to have to deal with it at night, too."

"You scared, girl. You scared! I told ya, ya gots to learn to fight. You learns to fight, then ya don't hafta all the time be scared."

"You make it sound so easy, but I'm not like you, Tashina."

Chapter Six

"You stick by me, girl! Long's you wit me, ain't nothin bad gonna happen to ya."

"Thanks, Tashina. You're a good friend. But I'm still scared."

Tashina walked to the door. She turned the knob, looked back, and shook her head. "What I'm gonna do wit you, girl?"

******

Sydney detected an I-told-you-so ring to Denise's voice on the phone. "Theresa Winter's mother called to decline the invitation for an interview. She said she heard from one of the other parents that there's a boarding school involved. 'Theresa is needed at home,' she said."

"That's disappointing. But I'm sure you have many single parents with full-time jobs and a lot of other children. We were bound to draw at least one."

"Theresa's an only child, Syd. Her mother's on welfare."

"Is the mother an invalid?"

"Far as I can tell, she's as able-bodied as I am."

"Hmmm. Did you tell her about the opportunity her daughter would be missing? Did you explain it, Denise?"

"She didn't give me much of a chance—just said, 'My daughter and I are very close, Ms. Hanover. Most people don't understand, but boarding school is out of the question, no matter what.'"

"She wouldn't even consider coming to an interview?"

"You got that right."

Sydney held the phone to his ear with his shoulder as he motioned to Kevin to pour more coffee. "I just don't understand it, Denise."

After Sydney hung up, he and Kevin had one of their familiar discussions about the illusive meaning of life.

******

The interview with Marvin and Carol Johnson, Karter's parents, was coming to an end. John had just asked if they had any reason why Karter shouldn't participate, when Karter knocked on the door and asked, "Are you ready for me yet?"

John exchanged a surprised look with Denise before he motioned toward an empty chair in the circle. "I guess we're ready. Sit down, Karter."

As soon as Karter was seated, Carol got up and walked over to where John was perched in his usual place on the edge of Denise's desk. She looked straight into John's eyes.

"I'm glad our boy will be in good hands—you being a man of the cloth and all. My husband is on the road a lot, and, well, Karter's on the streets more than he should be. He could use some spiritual guidance."

John turned his gaze toward Sydney. "This won't be a religious school, Mrs. Johnson. You see, it's an experiment to see how the children solve problems on their own."

"I'm sorry, Father. I simply cannot believe that a man of the cloth such as yourself would deny young people the spiritual guidance they so desperately need. I trust that in spite of the way things have been set up, you will do your Godly duty. May Jesus bless you for your goodness."

Karter rolled his eyes back in his head and sighed in exasperation. "Ma, sit down. You're embarrassing me."

Carol sat down, took a tissue from her purse, and dabbed at her eyes.

Marvin put his arm around Carol's shoulder. "The boy doesn't mean any harm, honey." Then he put his hand on his son's knee. "Karter, when will you understand? Your mother loves you. She has only your best interest at heart. You're always so critical..."

Karter pushed his father's hand away. "Don't I get a say? Don't I get to vote too?"

John cleared his throat. "I understand your concern, Mrs. Johnson. It's not easy raising children in these troubled times. It's difficult to be a parent." He turned to Karter. "It's difficult to be a kid, too."

John filled Karter in on the school and the experiment and asked him if he had any questions.

"I just want to know, Father, who else is gonna be there?"

"That's not something I can tell you at this time. Nothing's been settled yet—not for sure."

"I heard Tashina Jones is gonna be there. Maria Guliano, too."

"You know these girls, Karter? Would you object to their participation?"

"No, sir, not at all. I was just wondering."

"I can't give you that information, Karter. Do you have any other questions? Any reservations, reasons why you would not want to participate in this program?"

"No, sir, none at all. It sounds good to me! Us kids will be on our own, right?"

"Except, of course, for your school work."

Karter smirked and put a strut in his walk as he left the office with his parents.

When the Johnson family was safely out of earshot, Denise flashed a knowing look at her co-conspirators. "If I get to scratch one, Karter's my pick."

"You worry too much, Denise." Sydney snapped his fingers. "We're on our way. We have a plan, a school, a dorm, some teachers, and some students."

"Slow down, Syd. We got some problems here, guys." Denise took the chair behind her desk and motioned to the other chairs.

Sydney remained standing. "Why so serious, Denise? I thought we were moving along nicely."

"Your arithmetic isn't so good, Syd." Denise raised one eyebrow and cocked her head at Sydney. "Four commitments out of ten candidates so far, and only three more to interview?"

Sydney scratched his head, sat down, and took off his shoes. He rubbed his feet. "You'll have to go back and generate some more names from your database, Denise."

Denise stood up and groaned. "I guess I could do that."

"Sit down, Denise," John commanded. "I have an idea: I say we make it easy on ourselves. I say we take the other Stein twin."

Sydney felt his stomach churning. "We can't do that. It wouldn't be random."

"It would be a good thing to do." John walked over to the credenza and poured some water from the pitcher. "I liked Jenna's commitment to her sister. That showed character; it should be rewarded—respected. I say we take both of them."

Sydney drummed his fingers on the desk. "You just can't resist the impulse to meddle, can you, John?"

"I think John's right, Syd," Denise spoke with conviction in her voice. "The Stein girl seemed pretty firm about not going without her sister. If we have to replace her, we'd have to pick another name in addition to replacing the Austin boy and Theresa Winter. If our track record so far is any indication, there's bound to be some more holdouts. The Steins would agree. I say we go for it."

Sydney stood with his back to them, looking out the window.

John pleaded softly, "It would save a lot of time. What do you say, Syd?"

Sydney weighed his quest for purity of design against his impatience. He turned to face them. "I can see I'm outvoted. I guess we've got ourselves a set of twins."

"Double your pleasure, double your fun," Denise laughed. "That makes four girls and two boys so far. We still have to find a replacement for the Austin boy. I'll crank up my computer."

There was a knock at the door. The school secretary handed John a manila folder. "The Shastri family is here."

Sydney grabbed his shoes. "I thought we were finished for the day."

Denise shrugged. "I thought I had them down for next week. Well, they're here now. Might just as well get on with it. What do you say, guys?"

Sydney nodded.

John looked at his watch. "I can handle it. Show the parents in and have the boy wait, please."

Denise stood a good four inches taller than Rudyard Shastri. She offered him her hand. "I'm Denise Hanover. This is Sydney Schuster and Father John Murphy."

Rudyard extended his trembling hand toward Denise. "Parkinson's," he explained. "I have been afflicted with it for a very long time now."

"I'm sorry…"

"This is fine. We have become very accustomed to it. Could we continue, please?"

"Yes, of course. Please, have a seat."

Sydney gave his usual explanation. "Do you have any questions, Mr. and Mrs. Shastri?"

"This is a very generous thing you are doing, Mr. Schuster. My husband has been unable to work for many years. We are required to live on my income, and we still must honor our obligation to send money back to our less fortunate relatives in India. We would not be capable to provide such a thing for Mohandas."

"I take it that means you would like your son to participate."

"I have one question for you, Father Murphy, since you will be in charge of the school. The public school that

Mohandas currently attends does not provide an adequate academic challenge for him. I try to supplement for what is missing. We do lessons at home. Will your school provide him with a challenge?"

"We have two of the finest, most dedicated teachers available. Wayne Beemers will be teaching the social science and English courses. Jodi Maxstadt will handle science and math. With only ten students, I can assure you the teachers will be willing and able to address the need for enrichment, as well as the need for extra help."

Rannuka turned to face her husband. "What do you think about it, Rudyard?"

"It sounds like a fine thing to me, Rannuka."

"Well then, there is your answer, Mr. Schuster."

When Moe joined his parents in Denise's office, he sat quietly and waited to be addressed before speaking.

"I do have one question for you, Mr. Schuster."

"Yes."

"Would it be possible for my brother to also attend your school?"

Sydney held back a laugh. "Is he your twin?" He looked at John and Denise.

"No, sir, but we are very close in many ways."

"I'm sorry, son, I don't think that will be possible."

"I will be reluctant to leave Jahan behind, but I agree to participate."

The Shastri family was just out the door when John said to Denise and Sydney, "That is an incredibly beautiful woman."

Sydney raised one eyebrow. "I didn't think priests noticed things like that."

"I'm a priest, Syd, not a dead man."

Denise laughed. "Should we consider taking the boy's brother?

Sydney chuckled. "You already know the answer to that one, Denise."

*****

The peeling paint on the sign read: "Welcome to Mama's. Open 11:00 to 8:00 Daily."

Karter wondered what Mama's real name was. Everybody he knew, even the adults, called her Mama.

He peered through the smudgy window at the tables covered with cheap red-and-white-checked cloths and the outmoded cash register on the counter. The faded posters on the walls displayed "Authentic Mexican Foods: Tacos, Burritos, and Enchiladas." *They couldn't have gotten back without me seeing them.* He looked at his watch. *It's 10:30. They should be here by now.*

The large digital thermometer on the bank building across the street read 96 degrees. Karter wiped the sweat from his brow and searched for a sign of their rusted-out van. He looked at his watch again. *It sure would be great to have Eddie there with me. Between the two of us, we'd figure a way to get that prize money.*

When the van pulled up to the curb, Karter saw the sour look on Eddie's face. *Oh shit. I knew it. The old man's not going to let him go.* He heard Dezzie Cortez yelling.

"It was good enough for my mama. It's good enough for your mama. What makes you so all-the-time high and mighty? I don't like your smart-ass attitude, Eddie."

Dezzie cuffed Eddie on the side of his head. "You ain't been pulling your weight around here as it is. Now you want to be gone Monday through Friday? You know, sir, King Eddie, every time you ain't here to pull your weight, it's your mama and your sister that suffers."

Mama unlocked the restaurant. Karter followed them through the door, took a seat at one of the tables, and watched while Eddie's father started slamming dishes around.

"I ain't been well, Eddie. I can only do so much. I built this business from the hole in the wall your own grandma— bless her soul and may she rest in heaven— ran all by herself. It's for you, Eddie! You and Sophie. But you gotta work for it!"

"I hate it, Papa. I don't want it!" Eddie banged his fist on the counter. "Give it to Sophie!"

Dezzie raised his hand as if to hit the boy again. With his hand in midair, he glared at his son.

Eddie's eyes were shining with tears. "You know how many times I've been thinking about running, Papa? If you don't let me go, I don't know what I'm gonna do. Come on, Pop. You're not gonna stand in my way, are you?"

Sophie came out from the back room. She waved at Karter. "Let him go, Pop. I'll pick up the slack. I don't mind."

"What's the big deal?" Mama's voice boomed loud and husky. "Use some of the money you've been hoarding for his college fund. Hire a busboy. We can afford it. Let him go."

Eddie reeled around to look at his mother. "What college fund?" He turned back to face his father. "You mean you got me busing tables and scraping vegetables so you can put the nickels and dimes saved on a busboy into a college fund, and you won't let me have a chance at more money than this place could make in two lifetimes?"

Dezzie's shoulders sagged, and his voice cracked. "You and I both know that money's not gonna make it to no college fund, Eddie. You know about the virus. Thank the good Lord in heaven none of you got this thing. That's one bright spot anyway."

Dezzie's voice was a whisper now. "I need you, Eddie. The restaurant is a sure thing. You gotta learn the business. When I'm gone, the restaurant will at least keep a roof over your heads and food on the table."

Mama picked up a stack of plates and slammed them down on the counter. "You could live to be a hundred," she bellowed. "Having the virus's not the same as having AIDS! You make it bigger than life. The only thing you lost so far is your bedroom privileges."

Dezzie put his hands over his face to hide his tears.

"Let the boy go." Mama whispered, "Let him have his chance in life. We'll hire a busboy, Eddie."

"Thanks, Mama."

"How long you been sitting there, Karter?"

Karter stood up and looked down at his shoes. "I didn't hear nothing, Mrs. Cortez."

"You keep it that way, hear me?"

Chapter Six

"Yes, ma'am."

Mama picked up the phone and called Denise Hanover to let her know that Eddie would be delighted to take advantage of Mr. Schuster's generous offer.

*****

John walked into Denise's office and tossed his briefcase on a chair. "I saw a family sitting on the bench in the waiting area. Is the boy by chance our next potential student?"

Denise looked up from the papers she was flipping through. "Yes, Dennis Worchowski. Not exactly an honor-roll student, but not a bad kid. He comes from a good Catholic family." Denise winked at John.

"Just don't invite him to be an altar boy, John," Sydney teased as he poured himself a cup of coffee from the pot on the credenza. "Wouldn't want to single him out of the group."

"Don't worry, Syd. I know my boundaries, and I know the rules. Not every priest is just dying to get his hands on every young Catholic boy in sight, you know. The rumors are highly exaggerated. I'll go out and invite them in."

The sight of the boy sitting on the bench between his parents amused John. The crotch of Dennis's overalls hung down to his knees, his shirt was four sizes too big, and his shoes were untied. To John, he looked like a naïve buffoon, but with his peers, he fit right in.

Dennis Sr. and Dolly didn't take long to accept the offer on their son's behalf, and Dennis Jr. was called into the office.

"I understand they call you Demon." John motioned to the boy to sit down. "How did you get a name like that?"

Demon blushed. "When I was a little kid, they used to call me the little demon. I guess I got into a lot of mischief."

"You like the name?"

"It's better than Junior."

Demon slouched in his chair. His right leg jiggled up and down the whole time John was explaining about the school. "Dad! I thought we had it all planned out. You and me were gonna be partners."

"I had always thought that Demon would join me in the construction business someday, Father," Dennis Sr. explained.

"Dad, I don't hafta go to no college!" Demon looked at his father with pleading eyes and whined, "We had it all planned out."

"You could do both, son."

Demon scowled. "No, I couldn't."

John, Sydney, and Denise watched silently as Dennis Sr. and Dolly told Demon that they would not allow him to close off his options.

"We're very grateful for this opportunity, Mr. Schuster. Demon will be there."

*****

Chapter Six

It was dark when Melissa Whistler arrived at the back door of the house where she lived with her mother and three other siblings. She opened the door a crack and listened before entering. She shushed the dog, a sixty-five-pound boxer, and stuck a biscuit in his mouth before she tiptoed to the door of her mother's bedroom and peeked in.

The moonlight played tricks with the shadows on the snoring man that lay next to her mother. Melissa and her mother made eye contact, but no words were exchanged.

Melissa entered the room where she shared a bed with two much-younger girls and quietly closed the door behind her. She put a chair against the doorknob, climbed into the bed fully clothed, and felt under the mattress for the knife she kept hidden there. One of the little girls squirmed and moaned. "Shhh, Ginger, it's just me. It's OK, honey. Go back to sleep."

Melissa lay there with her eyes open. *Mama was so happy when Mr. Schuster told us about the school. I hope it works out.* She turned over and stroked her sister's hair. *Who's going to rescue Ginger when her turn comes?*

Chapter Seven
Orientation
September 1996

The ten students of the Schuster-Murphy Experimental School showed up at the parking lot of their old school at 6:45 A.M. that warm September morning, just as they had been instructed. They looked more like a group of kids going on a picnic in their shorts and T-shirts than students on the first day of school. They—suitcases, backpacks, and all—were herded onto a small yellow bus.

Karter, Eddie, and Demon grabbed seats in the back. Moe and Sam, for lack of a better choice in partners, sat together in the front of the bus. Tashina latched on to Maria like a nervous mother cat, pulling her into one of the middle seats. The twins sat together, across the aisle and one row behind Maria and Tashina. Melissa, in her usual position as the loner, chose a seat in the middle of the bus.

Even before the bus driver started the engine, Karter was organizing and strategizing. He stretched his legs out into the aisle and put his hands behind his neck. "There's better ways to spend that kinda money than just college. I figure I could breeze through a cheap and easy college. That'd take about half the money. Then I could use the other half for more interesting things."

Eddie poked Karter in the shoulder. "We got lucky. But we ain't got the money yet. If we don't play our cards right, we won't ever see it. Then I'll be stuck in the restaurant business with my old man for the rest of my life."

"You gotta think positive here, Eddie." Karter looked across the aisle at Demon. "What do you have to say, Demon?"

Demon shrugged.

Eddie poked Karter again. "First, we gotta get the money."

"Just stick with me. Pretty soon, we'll be running the place. We'll have the others doing what we tell them before the end of the week. We'll teach that Schuster guy a little something about cooperation if that's what he wants." Karter cracked his knuckles. "There's one good way to get cooperation: you take over."

"You make it sound easy."

"Piece of cake. See, here's how it works. You get to know them, how they function, what their weak points are. What are their strengths—the stuff you can use? The more stuff you get on them, the better. What do you know about Sam and Moe? I ain't seen them around much."

Eddie looked out the window as the bus pulled out of the lot and picked up speed. "Sam seems OK. He's one of them smart kids, but he's no wuss. Sam pulls off a lot of crap, but he never seems to get caught. Teachers like him."

"What about the little guy?"

"Moe?"

"Yeah, the brown-nosed reindeer." Karter snorted.

"Don't know him. He looks like a strong wind would blow him over. He shouldn't be too hard to handle."

Karter looked over at Demon. "We all know we could have ourselves a time with Maria. We gotta go slow, be careful—at first. I say we leave her be for the moment." Karter stretched his legs and rolled his shoulders. "I don't want to mess with the chocolate girl just yet. Tashina sticks to Maria like one of them Siamese twins. They've got one spine between them."

"Speaking of twins, them Stein twins don't look like twins." A sly grin crossed Karter's face as he sniggered. "Maybe they had different fathers."

*****

Melissa sat very still. Her eyes were on her book, but she wasn't reading. She was listening intently to the discussion going on in the seat behind her.

"Why couldn't we of left dem three stooges back at dat other school? Girl, we gonna have our hands full wit dem. I ain't worried bout me, but you so dumb bout stuff."

"Don't go asking for trouble, Tashina. If we just act polite and stay our distance, maybe they'll leave us alone."

"I ain't askin for no trouble, girl, but if trouble come lookin for us, I ain't runnin neither."

Tashina glanced across the aisle to where Sam and Moe were sitting. "What about dat Indian kid over there? He don't look like no Indian I ever saw. He don't talk like one, neither."

"You don't know everything, Tashina. Moe's not that kind of Indian. His family is from India. I've talked with him a couple of times. He seems nice."

"What kinda name is Moe? The only Moe I ever heard a is one of em three stooges, and I don't mean the ones in the back a the bus."

"It's short for Mohandras or Mohandes or something like that. His mother's real pretty. She wears one of those sheet-like things wrapped around her whole body. Moe says it's called a sorry or something."

"Ha, ha! A guy name a Moe whose mother wear a sheet. Ha, ha! Dat's a good one, Maria. I heard it all now."

"She's got a red mark on her forehead, almost just between her eyes but a little higher. She's nice too. Moe didn't tell me what the red mark means, but I know it's something special."

"How you get to know so much bout this Moe guy?"

"He shared his notes with me and stuff. Once, we went to his house to pick up a book I needed for a test. He even walked me home afterwards. 'The streets are not a very safe place for you, Maria. I will walk with you to your house.'" Maria tried to imitate Moe's accent.

"He really talk like dat? I thought he jus talked like dat for the benefit a impressin the teachers."

"I like Moe. I'm glad he was picked."

"Maria, you full a surprises, girl. You hidin some heat under them tight-fittin jeans you always wearin?"

Maria didn't answer.

"You can have it, then! There ain't gonna be no lil ol romance for this mama. No, I got me some plans, and they don't include no male-type figures. I worry bout you, girl."

"Moe's not like the others."

"We'll see."

Melissa stared out the window as Tashina and Maria continued chattering and the bus drove up the freeway ramp. *Those two are so different. I'd never figure them for friends.* She turned the page in her book, shifted in her seat, and strained her ears to pick up what she could from the twins. It was easier to get an occasional glimpse of them because they were across the aisle.

"I'm sure glad you're here with me, Bec."

"Yeah. Thanks, Jen. I owe you. Anything's better than that miserable house with the witch and the sticky, stinky half-kids. Dad sure got himself a mess when he got Erica." Becca looked out the window for a while before speaking again. "From the looks of things though," she nodded her head toward the back of the bus, "this might not be much of an improvement."

"So what? If we get the prize money, we'll be home free."

"*If* we get it. That Schuster guy must be crazy to think we're gonna all make nice with each other and show him how a bunch of kids can get along. I can't imagine making friends with any of them. We don't have anything in common with them. I mean *anything*, Jen."

"We all want the money. We've got that in common. All we have to do is figure out how to get along with each other for a year. That shouldn't be too tough." Jenna smirked. "We aren't going to have to marry any of them, you know."

"Ugh! Perish that thought!"

"Come on, they're not that bad." Jenna put her hand on Becca's shoulder.

"Except for that Karter character," Becca whispered.

"He wants the money, just like the rest of us. Try to be a little more positive, Becca."

"My little sister Jenna, always the optimist, always the peacemaker." Becca sighed. "I have to admit, I'd sure like to get my hands on that money."

Jenna looked out the window for a moment before turning back to her sister. "Maria seems nice."

"I suppose she's OK." Becca cocked her head and nodded at Melissa.

Melissa turned a page in her book and pretended not to notice.

"Life wouldn't be worth living," Becca took a deep breath and went on, "if we had to be stuck with a crowd like this for the rest of our lives. It's a good thing it's only a year." She looked across the aisle. "Who's the black girl?"

"Tashina Jones."

"Strange name. I've seen her in class, and I've heard rumors about her. My bead on it? She's nobody to mess with. I wonder if the new school's going to have metal detectors. I wouldn't put it past her to be carrying a blade."

"Shh," Jenna scolded. "Maybe Dad was right, Becca. We need to look out for each other first and worry about the money later. Keep your opinions to yourself. Your mouth could get us in a whole lot of trouble."

Becca shrugged. "Whatever."

"Keep it zipped. Talk to me when we're alone. At least until we figure things out a little better."

"All right, all right. I got it, OK?"

Jenna moaned. "Sure wish we were still living with Mom and going to our old school."

Becca was quiet for a few moments before Melissa heard her say, "That one with the book in her face, Melissa—she keeps looking back at us."

"Becca, shh." Jenna rolled her eyes.

Melissa made a point not to look in their direction again.

Eavesdropping on Sam and Moe was easy. They were sitting directly in front of her. Melissa watched as Moe nodded toward the twins. "How do you think it happened that both of them were chosen?"

Sam reached for the candy bar in his pocket. "I don't know. My dad says people try too hard to connect the dots and find something that's not there. He says coincidences happen all the time. But I've got to admit, that would be some coincidence, both of them being picked."

"I guess if you are a rich man, then you get to do the choosing, and that Mr. Schuster must be a very rich man. It doesn't matter to me about it. Their good fortune is their good fortune, and I have my own."

"So what do you think we have to do to get it—the money, I mean?" Sam broke the candy bar and handed half to Moe.

"I think we are obliged to solve our own problems. That could be very difficult."

"Yeah, I know what you mean. You can't get along with some people no matter what. Like my little brother—he's such a pest."

"For me, it is very different. There is great trust between my brother and myself. I tell him many things."

Melissa looked through the window as the bus pulled onto the large, black-topped parking lot. There were three brick buildings, a school, a house, and a two-story building that she figured for the convent. *I thought there was supposed to be a church here. Where is it?*

Father John was in front of the convent, waving and calling a welcome as the teenagers scrambled off the bus.

Melissa hung back and watched Karter climb out of the bus last, with his backpack slung over one shoulder and a smart-aleck look on his face. The others turned around and looked back when he shouted, "Hey man, look at this, would ya? This is the boonies." The rest just stood there looking as he strode past them. "Real, honest-to-goodness B.F.E." He held his hands over his belly and grunted as though he had cramps. "Where's the outhouse?"

Eddie and Demon gave out the requisite belly laughs as they followed Karter.

Melissa moved up to the head of the group, two steps behind Father John, who was talking as he led the entourage into the convent dining room. "You all know why you're here, what you're supposed to accomplish, but you're still kids and this is still a school. There are rules."

John stood at the head of the feudal oak dining table. The table would have looked more at home in a cavernous stone castle than it did crammed into the stingy space provided by the budget of middle-class parishioners.

Melissa didn't want to get stuck with the last empty seat. She quickly took one next to Father John and hoped for the best. The rest filed in, deposited their suitcases and backpacks on the floor, and sat stiffly in chairs too vast for their half-grown adolescent bodies.

"Each of you will have a room of your own. Feel free to put pictures on the walls and decorate with personal items of your choice. You can lock your door for privacy or for safety if you like."

Melissa had been sitting rigidly upright, but when she heard the part about locking doors and privacy, she relaxed her shoulders a little and sat back in her chair.

John continued, "Only one student at a time is allowed inside a locked room. Your house parents, Mr. and Mrs. Sweeney, have a master key to be used in case of an emergency; otherwise, your privacy will be respected. Bedrooms are for sleeping and studying." John walked around the table.

Melissa scanned the faces of her classmates and wondered what was on Karter's mind.

"Do your socializing downstairs—downstairs in one of the two living areas or the dining room. Both living areas have a television hooked up to cable; you'll have to agree on what programs to watch in your free time. There's a pingpong table in one. Any questions so far?"

Karter laughed. "Yeah. How come those twins don't look alike?"

Melissa figured Karter was expecting a good laugh. Instead, he got an icy stare from Father John and piercing silence from the rest of the group. Even Eddie rolled his eyes.

"Just kidding." Karter turned the palms of his hands toward the ceiling. "It's a joke, you guys." His face turned red, and he kept his mouth shut during the rest of the orientation.

"Ten o'clock is curfew," John continued without responding to Karter's crude joke. "There will be bed checks. One person per room, that's the rule. Violating this rule could get you expelled from the school, and you all know what that means. You've signed on for a year. If anybody leaves, all will lose the prize. Mr. Schuster was very emphatic: All will win or none will win. There you have it, my little leprechauns. Any questions?" John stared directly at Karter.

"In a moment we'll go upstairs, and you can put your things away and settle in. One last thing: There are three large bathrooms equipped with a tub and shower. One is assigned to the girls, one to the boys, and the other is for Mr. and Mrs. Sweeney—you'll get to meet them later today. The doors are clearly marked. The girls' bathroom is off-limits to boys, and vice versa." John looked at Karter again. "Are there any questions about that?"

Karter kept his head down.

"Then you can go upstairs now, choose your rooms, and freshen up. We'll reconvene back here for school programs and schedules in about thirty minutes."

The second floor had been altered to accommodate its new tenants. A wall between two of the twelve identical bedrooms had been torn down to provide more appropriate space for the house parents. Crosses and holy pictures had been removed, and the walls were freshly painted. The furniture, however, remained the same as it had been when the Sisters of Notre Dame occupied these quarters. Each meager room was equipped with a cot, a small chest of drawers, a desk (sporting a brand new computer), and a closet.

Melissa waited until all the rooms had been chosen. She paid close attention to who took which rooms. Then she checked the lock on her door before she put her things away.

When she joined the group downstairs, Melissa heard Karter telling his buddies that the computer in his room was locked out of his favorite porn sites.

Father John was handing out the written agenda.

Demon Worchowski took one look at the schedule and muttered under his breath, "Damn, this is gonna be just like regular school." He kicked at a table leg.

Eddie punched Demon's shoulder gently. "What'd you expect, Demon? They're getting us set for college."

Demon pushed Eddie away. "Who needs it?" He kicked the table again and addressed his comments directly to Father John. "Why can't I just be a frickin carpenter? Why does everybody have to run my life?"

The din of voices in the room subsided. All eyes jumped to Demon. Melissa wondered why Father John didn't respond to Demon's outburst. *I guess they were serious about us solving our own problems,* she thought, as she watched Eddie make an effort to comfort Demon.

Eddie whispered, "There'll be plenty of time to shoot some hoops after classes, Demon. How about it?"

"Yeah, yeah, OK. It can't be worse than before." Demon's shoulders drooped as he re-evaluated the schedule.

Moe asked a couple questions about curriculum, grades, books, and testing procedures,

Becca wanted to know if there would be a fast-track program for students who were serious about finishing high school early. She had questions about transferring credits earned here to apply toward a magnet school.

"Now, why didn't I think a dat!" Tashina punched Becca on the arm. "You gots brains, girl, and you usin em. You and me, we gonna get along jus fine. What's you name again?"

"Becca—Becca Stein."

"I'm gonna member dat one."

In her iciest voice, Becca responded, "Maybe it would be better if you would learn to speak the English language first...*girl*."

Melissa overheard Tashina whisper to Maria something about "no provocation" and "jus bein friendly." She saw Jenna silence Becca with a look, and she wondered how

Chapter Seven

long Jenna would be able to keep Becca and Tashina from tangling with each other.

*****

That night, after bed check, Melissa watched from her cracked-open bedroom door as Becca dragged her cot mattress into Jenna's room.

She locked herself in her own room and had the first good night's sleep since she couldn't remember when.

Chapter Eight
Settling In
September-October 1996

Karter was chomping down his baloney sandwich at the lunch table. "Maria," he hollered, "get me another cola." He was in a mood to regain the status he'd lost during orientation.

Tashina grabbed Maria's arm to hold her back and shouted at Karter, "Get it yourself, Karter. She ain't your nigger."

Maria pulled away from Tashina's grip. "Never mind, Tashina," she whispered as she headed toward the kitchen.

Karter gave Tashina a sly smirk and took another large bite of his sandwich. He chuckled as Tashina took her sandwich and stomped out of the room.

When Maria returned with Karter's cola in hand, Karter smiled and said, "Thank you, Maria."

He looked to his buddies, who nodded their heads in approval, and watched Maria sit down to finish her lunch quietly, albeit quickly.

Karter had cautioned his buddies to lay low on Maria, but he couldn't resist giving her the old evil eye every now and again. She got all flustered and tried to make believe she didn't notice. *I'll bet I just give that girl goose bumps all over her body*, he thought. *You can see her just a-shakin.*

With Maria, it was a game for Karter. When it came to real heavy-duty fantasizing, however, it was Tashina that was in his dreams, not Maria.

Later that evening, after dinner, Karter was lying on his cot, alone in his room. He got up and paced in a circle, peered out the window, looked at his watch, and lay back on the bed again. Within seconds, he was back up, checking that his door was locked. He dug a prescription bottle from its hiding place (carefully tucked under his underwear in the bottom bureau drawer), dumped out the pills, counted them, and put them back in the bottle. *He used to flush these little gems down the toilet—Demon's so dumb. It took me to educate him about the value of medical science, and the street value of Ritalin.*

He took his cell phone from the bottom drawer and punched in a number from the memory.

Rick Guliano picked up on the other end. "Yeah?"

"You're gonna have to drive out to the Falls if you want this stuff before the weekend." Karter rolled the bottle around in his hand as he spoke.

"Nah, I got stuff going on here. I'll catch you on the weekend when you're back in town." Rick hung up.

Karter slammed the phone down on the bed and stormed out of his room. "F this crap!" Halfway down the hall he turned around and stomped back. He kicked his bedroom door open and went in to return the phone and the Ritalin to their hiding place. When he got back to the hall, he saw Eddie and Demon heading for the stairs. "Hey, you guys, come here. I wanna talk to you."

When Eddie and Demon were inside Karter's room, Karter locked the door.

"Hey man," Eddie protested, "you want to get us all kicked out? You know it's against the rules to lock the door with more than one of us inside."

"Since when were you so concerned with rules?"

"Since I got a chance for a butt-load of money, that's since when."

"All right, all right. Flip the lock, but the door stays shut. There ain't no rule against closed doors that I know of."

Eddie fired Karter a caustic look and unlocked the door. Demon sat cross-legged on Karter's bed. Karter straddled the desk chair, and Eddie sat on the floor.

"Get your feet off my bed, man."

Demon groaned and put his feet down.

Eddie moved next to Demon on the cot. "What's up, Karter?"

Karter tapped his fingers on the desk. "I got this idea. We gotta develop a plan to convince the Schuster guy we're all getting along."

Eddie and Demon nodded in agreement.

"See, I been thinking. It ain't so much about getting along as it is about *telling* him we're getting along." He raised his eyebrows. "Get my drift?"

Eddie frowned. "No, I don't get it. What do you mean, tell him we're getting along?"

"It's a simple concept, Eddie. Use your head." Karter spoke very slowly. "I figure it would be easier to get everybody to *say* we're getting along than to actually do it."

"Get real, Karter. You're saying we get everybody to pull off a colossal lie?" Eddie drew his elbows tight to his body, put his palms up, and shrugged his shoulders. "How are we going to convince anyone that you and Tashina Jones like each other, for example?"

"I can handle Tashina." A wee smile crossed Karter's face as a picture of him *getting along* with Tashina flashed through his head. "We're more alike than you might think."

Eddie's eyes lit up. "So we just do business as usual and then at the end, when they ask us, we just tell them we like each other. That what you mean, Karter?"

"That's cooperation, ain't it? We tell Schuster what he wants to hear. He gets to feel like some kinda hero, and we get the money. That way, everybody's happy."

"Way to go, man." Eddie gave him a high-five.

Demon shook his head. "Yeah, everybody but me. I don't give a frickin crap about the money. It's got strings. I'd be better off if we failed this dumb test."

Eddie punched Demon hard on the shoulder. "We all get it, or none of us do." He scowled at Demon. "You ain't gonna sabotage us, are you, chum?"

Demon looked at the floor. "I ain't nobody's martyr, Eddie." His voice was barely audible.

Karter's eyes narrowed into mean-looking slits and his veins stuck out as he grabbed Demon's shirt collar and threatened, "You make me lose a half a million dollars, and you ain't never gonna make it to your destination, Mr. Dennis Worchowski. That is, unless your destination is an early arrival in the sweet hereafter. I won't be the only one out after your butt, either."

Demon glared back at Karter. "Fine. I get the point, Karter. I'm a martyr. Just tell me what you want me to do."

Karter let go of his grip on Demon's collar and faked a smile. He ran his knuckles across Demon's head in a mock playful manner. "A little *cooperation*, Demon. That's all I'm asking."

"Yeah, yeah. I get the picture." Demon slumped down on the bed.

Karter's nostrils flared as he snarled, "Just the same, I'll be keeping my eye on you."

$$*****$$

While Karter was keeping his eye on Demon, Tashina Jones was keeping her eye on Maria and Moe. She shook her head. *I warned her. I said, Girl, you gonna be sorry. How you spek me to help ya if ya ain't never gonna listen to me? The hell wit it!*

Tashina pulled an oversized red sweatshirt over her head, smoothed her hair, and went looking for the blond twin—the bigger one. She knocked on Becca's door.

"Hi, Becca," she said. She knew better than to call her "girl."

"Hi." Becca surprised Tashina with a shy smile.

Tashina was speechless. Her mouth hung open for a moment before her words found their way out. "Wanna talk?"

"Sure, come on in." Becca stepped aside.

The two girls faced each other just inside the open door. Tashina wasn't going to let the unexpectedly friendly welcome interrupt her well-rehearsed speech.

"Look, Becca, I likes to put my cards on the table right upfront-like, I figure you for a smart person. Whether you knows it or not, I'm a smart person myself. The way I talk don't mean nothin. It's jus a front, a way to get people to keep their distance."

"It works."

"Yeah, well. Maybe sometime I don't want *some* people to keep their distance." Tashina looked Becca in the eyes and waited for a response.

Becca had a puzzled look on her face. "So, what did you want to talk about?"

"Do ya mind if I sit down here on your bed?"

"No, that's OK. Go ahead." Becca closed the door and sat on her desk chair.

"Where your sister at? You two all the time together?"

"Even twins have to get away from each other sometimes. She's in her room studying for the history test."

Tashina rubbed the back of her neck and stretched out. "Sometime I wish I had a sister. I got my mama and grandma. They's pretty good company."

"Was there something special you wanted to talk about, Tashina?"

"Yeah. Member our first day here—when Father John was tellin us bout classes and alladat stuff? You mentioned somethin bout gettin outta high school fast. Can ya do dat? I mean, go through in less than four years and still get to go to college?" Tashina crossed her legs and sat Indian-style on Becca's cot. "I gots plans for me, jus like you gots plans for you, and I'm in jus as much a hurry as you."

"Sure you can." Becca's smile was warmer, more genuine than the tentative one she gave Tashina at the door. "All you have to do is take on more credits at a time. It's a lot of hard work, but it can be done if you're smart enough. I'm going to do it. I know lots of kids who did high school in three years."

Tashina nodded. "I think I could do it, too." She uncrossed her legs and sat up straight. "Most a the time, I be bored wit the stuff they gives us. And I sure ain't gonna get myself all tangled up wit some lil romance jus for the distraction. I don't do no drugs, neither."

Becca shook her head and pursed her lips. "I think you mean any—any drugs, not no drugs, and it's either, not neither."

Tashina took a deep breath and squinted her eyes. "Well, I ain't gonna change the way I be talkin til I'm situated in a safer place dan where I been alla my life."

Becca opened the drawer of the desk and took out two Snickers bars. She handed one to Tashina. "Want one?"

"Thanks. You OK in my book, Becca."

The two girls smiled sheepishly at each other as they munched their candy bars.

"Before we can discuss the next phase of our lives, Tashina, we have to figure out how to finance it. Got any ideas—besides just keeping ourselves safe and clean, that is?"

"Not yet, but I think Karter Johnson and his two stooges ain't up to no good. Karter called a meetin with alla us at seven tomorrow."

"I'm not sure I want to trust my fate to that bunch." Becca sighed. "Maybe we girls need to do some organizing of our own."

Tashina clapped her hands together and snapped her fingers. "Dat's zactly what I gots on my mind. Maybe we talk different, but we think the same. I think we gonna get along jus fine, girl."

Becca rolled her eyes and sighed. "You're going to have to stop with the 'girl' stuff, Tashina. It's a real turn-off."

"I can do dat." Tashina grinned. "But you gonna hafta make some concessions, too. You gonna hafta stop alla time correctin me—specially when there's others listenin. Works both ways, ya know."

"Deal."

The two shook hands.

Becca finished the last bite of her candy bar and tossed the wrapper in the basket. "So what are we going to do about Karter?"

"Together, we can take him on. I mean alla us," Tashina hesitated, "girls."

Becca laughed. "We got *girl* power."

Tashina jumped off the cot, flung her arms above her head, and whirled like a dervish. "Girl power! Girl power! Go! Go! Go!"

When Becca stopped laughing, she grabbed Tashina by the shoulders and gently pushed her down on the bed.

Tashina admitted she needed the rescue. She took some time to regain her equilibrium before Becca got back to business.

"We need to get started. I can talk to my sister. Can you handle Maria?"

"I think so." Tashina frowned. "What we gonna do bout Melissa? I ain't so sure bout her."

"Maybe we should both talk to her."

Becca and Tashina waited in the hall for a full three minutes according to Becca's watch before Melissa opened her door a crack and peered out at them.

Tashina stood behind Becca. Their agreed-upon strategy was to let Becca do the talking, unless things didn't go well. Then Tashina was supposed to chime in for support.

Becca's voice was friendly. "Hi, Melissa. Can we come in?"

Melissa kept her firm hold on the door. "It's late."

"We won't take much time, Melissa. It's important."

"I guess so." Melissa sighed and stepped aside.

The three girls endured a few moments of awkward silence before Tashina got impatient with Becca's slow pace. She put the palms of her hands up and shrugged her shoulders. "Ah, Melissa, do you spose we could sit down?"

Melissa cleared some books and papers off her cot and sat down. Tashina sat next to her and Becca took the chair.

Becca used her most somber voice. "Look, Melissa, we need your help. Karter's called a meeting for tomorrow night, and we think he's up to one of his schemes to take over leadership. With him in charge of things, there's no telling what might happen."

Melissa had a blank expression on her face. "I'd rather not get involved in anything."

"We've got way too much at stake to leave things in the hands of Karter Johnson. Tashina and I have been talking." With a sideways glance at Tashina, she continued, "We *girls* have got to stick together if we're going to stop Karter from taking over."

Melissa answered in a monotone. "I probably won't even go to Karter's meeting."

Tashina stood up and put her hands on her hips. She glared at Melissa through wild eyes. "Ya know what he been sayin bout you, girl? He been sayin it's the quiet ones be best in bed." Tashina squinted and pointed her finger for dramatic effect. "Ya sleepin wit him, girl?"

She waited a second for the response she was pretty sure she wouldn't get. "If ya are, dat's none a our business, but if ya ain't, ya gonna need some heavy-duty protectin. Learn who your friends are, girl. Let's go, Becca. We done wit our business here."

After they left Melissa's room, Becca whirled around at Tashina. "What did you do that for? You probably frightened that poor kid half to death."

"Ya want her at dat meetin, don't ya? Ya might be smart in a lotta ways, Becca Stein, but ya jus gonna have to trust lil ol Tashina Jones sometime. Dat girl know a thing or two. A little fear can get ya lookin round for who your friends be. See ya tomorrow, Becca. Nice talkin wit ya."

Tashina strutted off in the direction of her room, slightly smug at her glimpse of Becca standing still with her mouth open.

****

The Sweeneys had given Maria and Moe permission to use the convent kitchen after six.

Maria was stirring the fudge on the stove. Moe gently stroked her hair from behind. "You know very much about cooking, Maria."

"Been cooking since I was nine or ten. That's why I always had to leave school right away. I had to start supper before my mom got home from work."

"I thought it was me that you were avoiding."

"Nah." Maria gave Moe a reassuring smile. "It didn't have anything to do with you. I would have loved to spend time with you, Moe."

"Really? Let me help you to clean this mess, Maria." He grabbed a towel and wiped the counter. "In my house, my brother and I, we are not allowed to be in the kitchen. It seems to me like the food just appears—like some kind of magic happened behind the closed door."

Maria handed Moe a chopping board, a bag of nuts, and a knife. "Want to chop these?"

"I would be happy to do it."

"You won't see guys in the kitchen at my house either— not when there's work to be done. It's not like they're not allowed. The kitchen is where we do our eating. It's more like they choose not to participate—except for the eating, that is. They do plenty of that."

"In my house, my mother is expected to do everything. I do not like it that way. I thought it was different in American families." He handed Maria the chopped nuts, and she stirred them into the fudge.

"My mom works just as hard as my dad all day, but when they get home, my dad gets to sit down and have a beer. He settles himself into his La-Z-Boy and watches television. My mom gets to do the laundry or whatever else needs doing."

"I guess it is really not so different. In my culture, women are supposed to wait on the men and even the boys. My mother, she is very beautiful, and she is also very smart. When she is at her place of employment, she is treated with much respect and dignity. She tells the others what to do, even the men."

"My mom tells my dad what to do. He doesn't listen so good, though—on second thought, he usually ends up doing what Mom says, except for chores, that is."

Maria poured the fudge into a dish and scraped the pan with a spatula. Moe put his hand on her cheek and gently turned her face toward his. "Maria, there is something very wrong about the ways in which men treat women. I would never treat you like that."

Maria's heart was beating so hard and so fast she wondered if Moe could see it thumping right through her shirt.

Chapter Eight

Moe continued peering into Maria's eyes and stroking her cheek. "When my mother comes home from her place of employment, she puts on her sari and she becomes my father's servant. She props his head on a pillow and rubs his feet. I don't like it."

Maria moved away from Moe's hand and grabbed the popcorn pan from the shelf, immediately pouring the oil and the corn into it. She handed it to Moe. "I think things are about to change at my house. You should have seen the look on my little brother's face when Mom told him to clear the table and help his sister with the dishes—shake the pan or the popcorn will burn." Maria stood at the sink with the water running. She was cleaning the fudge pan. "If you want my opinion, I think things should have changed a long time ago—before my brother Rick got too big for his britches. My mom says, 'Like father, like son.'"

"I am not going to become a man like my father." Moe shook the pan on the stove. "My father has the disease called Parkinson's. It makes his hands and arms shake. He would like everybody to believe that he is an invalid. I looked it up in the medical dictionary. I understand that he is a very sick man. I do not believe that he is an invalid."

Maria took the pan from Moe and poured the popcorn into a bowl. "Should we put some melted butter on it?"

"That would be very good."

"Do you have popcorn at your house?"

"No, we eat very differently. But I like popcorn—and I like you, Maria." Moe put his hands on Maria's shoulders and turned her to face him. "I like you very much, Maria."

"I like you, too, Moe."

Maria felt her face flush as she and Moe hugged one another.

Moe gently pushed Maria's head back and looked at her face. "I would like to kiss you, Maria—if that would be agreeable."

Maria had been kissed before, but she'd never been asked before. It was the sweetest, gentlest kiss she'd ever had.

After that one brief kiss, Maria gently pushed Moe away and salted the popcorn. Moe stood back and looked at her with an admiring expression. "You are very beautiful, Maria." A smile slowly erupted across his face. "I like to say your name."

Maria blushed. "You'll probably make some nice girl a good husband some day, Moe."

"That is another thing, Maria—another thing about my culture. They have already chosen a bride for me. She is just a little girl in diapers. We will not be able to meet with one another until just before the wedding."

"No!" Maria wiped her hands on a towel and looked directly at Moe. "You're kidding. Really? That's barbaric. Everyone should get to pick who they want to marry."

Maria saw the tears forming in Moe's dark brown eyes. "What if I don't like her, Maria? What if she is fat and ugly and has pimples all over her face? What will I do then?"

Maria brushed a tear from Moe's cheek. "It's not right. Everybody should be allowed to pick who they want to marry."

"If I could choose right now, Maria, I would choose you."

"I'd pick you too, Moe. I told Tashina she was wrong about you. You're not like the rest."

This time Moe didn't ask. Maria felt her body quivering and her heart racing as she and Moe shared a long and passionate kiss. Then she gently pushed his groping hands away. "Sam and the twins are watching a movie. Should we give them some of this fudge?"

"That would be a very good thing to do."

*****

The next day Karter had a confident bounce in his step as he did his campaigning. "Hey, Sammy, my boy. Did you hear about the meeting tonight? We're making a plan to secure that prize money. I'm counting on your support, man. When we get to the part of showing hands, I'm expecting yours to be up for me."

"Yeah sure, Karter, no problem."

When Karter saw Melissa off in a corner with her nose in a book, he strolled over, pushed her hair behind her ear, and whispered, "You'd better be voting for me tonight, little quiet girl."

Melissa didn't respond.

Karter was gratified to see her shiver when he turned back to wink.

He shot Demon a chilling look in passing. "I got my eye on you, Buddy Boy."

*****

Tashina and Maria decided to go for a walk during the lunch break.

"What your friend Moe say bout what Karter gots up his sleeve, beside a smelly armpit?"

"Moe doesn't get involved in all that stuff, Tashina. You're wrong about him. He's not one of them. He's not like them."

Tashina smirked. "He may be little, but he still a male-type, ain't he? He gots his brain in his pants, and his hands in his pockets, don't he?"

"Oh, what's the use? You think all boys are bad just because they're boys." Maria stopped walking and put her hands on her hips. "Well, let me tell you something, Tashina Jones. Boys are people, too! They're not all alike. What's eating you, anyway?"

"Whooo-eee. Look at you, girl! Standin up for yourself like dat." Tashina slapped her thigh and laughed. "I jus hope you can keep dat up, girl. We gonna need all the spunk we can muster if we gonna keep Karter Johnson from gettin too big for his britches or fore you know it, he'll have alla us kissin his nasty little butt and thankin him for the favor a bein allowed to do it."

*****

Tashina was furious when she saw Karter standing at the head of the table, his thumbs hooked into his side pockets—taking over the leadership role at the meeting as though it were his preordained right.

"The only person missing from this here meeting is Melissa. I say we—"

"We ain't startin til we all here," Tashina yelled as she stood facing him from the other end of the table.

"The little quiet girl's never got anything important to say anyway, Tashina. You can fill her in on what we decide in the morning," Karter sneered.

Tashina screamed, "Who made you the boss? Ya goin a little too quick here, don't ya think, Mr. Karter Johnson? I don't hear no votin goin on."

Becca chimed in, "She's right, Karter. I say we wait for Melissa."

"Go get her, then. I can't wait all night. We got business here!"

Tashina let Becca stare Karter down this time. *May as well show those boys dat more than one a us girls can stand up to em.*

Tashina wasn't surprised when Jenna rescued her twin by giving in to Karter's demand.

"I'll go get her." Jenna headed for the door.

Karter threw his hands in the air. "I guess we're waiting on the little quiet one, then." He sat down and tapped his fingers on the table.

Tashina walked over to where Karter was sitting and folded her arms across her chest. "Yeah, Karter, we waitin til alla us is here. You got a problem wit dat?"

"I already said I'd wait, Tashina. Keep your pants on."

Tashina stomped back to her seat, but she kept the scowl firmly fixed on her face.

When Jenna came back with Melissa, Karter took a cheap shot. "I hope we didn't interrupt your beauty rest, Melissa. Just what do you do in your room all the time, little quiet girl—play with yourself?"

Eddie stifled a laugh.

Tashina's temples pulsed. She was halfway out of her chair, when Jenna shot her a look that said keep it zipped, and Tashina forced herself to sit down.

"Sorry," Melissa muttered as she slumped into her place at the table.

"OK. Are we all here? Do we agree on that subject?" Karter looked around the room at his classmates.

Just then Mr. Sweeney poked his head into the room. Karter looked at him and said, "Do you mind, Mr. Sweeney? We got some private business going on here."

"It was getting a little loud...."

"OK, Mr. Sweeney. Not to worry. We'll keep it down, OK?"

After Mr. Sweeney left, Karter got back to his agenda. "Do we all agree on the purpose of this here meeting?"

Becca answered, "Why don't you just refresh our memories, Karter?"

Karter turned his attention to Demon. "We all want the prize, don't we?"

Demon averted his eyes. "Just get on with it, Karter. You don't have no dissenters here," he mumbled.

"Glad to hear it, Buddy Boy." Karter looked around at the others. "Way I see it; we've all been looking at this thing the wrong way. They told us we had to find a way to get along with each other. Think about that very carefully—they didn't say we had to *like* each other."

Eddie stood up in support of Karter. "Think about that for a minute. They didn't say we had to *like* each other. That's a very important point."

"Sit down, Eddie. I can handle this."

Eddie slouched down in his seat.

"They might have it in their heads that way, but they didn't *say* it. They didn't put it in writing. For example, as my good friend Eddie over here so aptly pointed out to me," Karter paused to look at Tashina, "me and Tashina here, we ain't never gonna *like* each other."

"I gotta give it to ya, Karter. You got dat part right." *The day I be chummy wit you, Karter Johnson, is the day they be takin me to the loony bin in a straitjacket.*

Karter's hand brushed his crotch, and he went on. "If we can just agree on a simple thing, we can save a lot of trouble. All we gotta do is convince them we're all palsey-walsey here."

"How we gonna do dat, Karter? Ain't nobody gonna believe we's palsey-walsey."

"Tashina, I ain't never questioned your intelligence. Use your brain here. They want cooperation. Let's give them cooperation."

Eddie gave out a cheer. "Yeah!"

Tashina glared at Karter. "I'm listenin."

"Here's how it goes. We all agree to tell them what they want to hear. If that ain't cooperation, I'm missing something here. It's like we're a team. We don't hafta be special friends with everybody on the team; we just gotta agree on a strategy to win the game."

Tashina caught Jenna rolling her eyes at Becca. "You think this is a game, Karter?" Jenna asked.

"Yeah, a game between us and them."

"Mr. Schuster said that everybody wins or nobody wins."

"Give me a little credit here, Jenna. I thought this thing through very carefully. Listen to me. We *will* all be winners. There are some very crucial points to understand here. It's not what the thing is; it's what the thing looks like that counts."

Tashina kept her mouth shut. Jenna had a good hold on the group's attention, and Tashina wasn't about to waste that good girl power if she didn't have to.

"Mr. Schuster is willing to give us a lot of money and a better crack at life if we can figure out a way to be friends and get along with each other," Jenna continued. "You just lost me, Karter. How is he going to be a winner if we just *pretend* to be friends?"

"I already covered that point, Jenna. Weren't you listening? It's a very simple thing. It's not what the thing *is* that counts; it's what he *thinks* the thing is that's important. We just tell him what he wants to hear, and he thinks he's a winner."

Eddie jumped out of his seat and gave Karter a high-five. "We make him think he's a winner, and we win!"

"Right! You got it, Eddie. You understand where I'm coming from. He wins because he thinks we're all palsey-walsey, not because we are. And he gets to feel good about giving a bunch of money to some poor slob disadvantaged kids. He gets to think he's discovered the meaning of life, for Christ's sake. It don't get much better than that for an old guy like him. We'd be doing him a favor!"

Tashina kept her mouth shut. *What he be sayin makes some kinda weird sense, but somethin's wrong. I gots to figure it out, fore I talk.*

"Do I understand you right, Karter?" Jenna pushed. "All we've got to do is pretend that we're friends for the next seven months and we get the prize? That's it?"

"Yeah. Congratulations, Jenna, you got it." Karter stood up, put his hands in his back pockets, and walked around the table. "We all just go about our business as usual, and then at show-and-tell time we tell them we're all buddy-buddy. We protect each other, cover each other's backs. You know, like teamwork."

Tashina sprang out of her chair and whirled around to face Karter as he was passing behind her. "Lil ol Tashina Jones here got some questions for ya, Karter Johnson. And your answers better be good!"

She spat her words in Karter's face. "Ya mean ya can jus go on takin advantage a my friends? Ya can jus go on bullyin Maria and Melissa here, scarin the pants off em? Ya gets to go on insultin em every chance ya gets and we jus sposed to sit back and keep are mouths shut? And then we sposed to lie bout it in the bargain? I don't think so. Dat ain't gonna work, Karter Johnson, no way!"

Karter walked back to his place at the table. "You got a better idea?"

"I gotta hand it to ya. Some things ya be sayin make sense here, but some don't. One thing for certain: We needs to get ourselves organized, and we needs to get ourselves a leader. I say we use the good ol democratic process. Jus in case you didn't know bout it, women gets to vote now. Do I have nominations from the floor?"

Becca nominated Tashina. Eight mouths dropped open when Melissa Whistler quickly seconded. Tashina gave Melissa a broad-faced grin, and Melissa responded with a shy smile of her own.

Tashina wasn't surprised when Eddie nominated Karter and Demon seconded.

The hands went up: four for Tashina and four for Karter.

When Tashina saw Moe's hand go up for Karter, she poked Maria on the arm. "Thought ya said he ain't like alla rest."

Maria rolled her eyes. "Get off it, Tashina."

Karter, the budding politician, congratulated Tashina on her victory with the girls. "I knew we were two of a kind, and I mean that as a sincere compliment." He winked at Tashina.

"Don't flatter yourself. It ain't becomin."

Tashina primed for the fight she knew was coming.

Chapter Nine
Thanksgiving Break
November 1996

John peered out the window over his desk. He'd been waiting a full hour for Sydney to show up. He picked up a folder, opened it and paged through its contents, closed it, and tossed it down on the desk. He looked out the window again, took a sip of his cold coffee, and made a face. When John saw Sydney slide into the lot, he raised his eyebrows. *What's this? Sydney's driving—and Denise is with him.*

"What a pleasant surprise to see you here, Denise." John greeted her with a hug, giving Sydney a questioning look over her shoulder.

Sydney grinned sheepishly. "She's taking me to Door County for a little holiday after we've finished our business."

"I can't think of a more pleasant way to spend a weekend." John winked at Denise. "In the company of such a lovely woman? You're a lucky man, Syd."

"Mr. World Traveler here's never been to Door County. He's traveled all over Europe and been to parts of Asia, but he's never seen Wisconsin's Pride. Can you believe that, John?"

"Good to see you teaching Mr. Serious how to loosen up a little. Can I interest you in some coffee? I sure could use some." John called to Mrs. McPhearson to make a fresh pot. "Sit down, make yourselves comfortable."

John took the chair behind his desk. Denise and Sydney settled into the two across from him.

"I'm glad you're here, Denise. Maybe you can talk some sense into him. He thinks I'm jeopardizing the integrity of the experiment. I say we don't have the right to sacrifice a student's academic needs. You're an educator; you know what I mean."

"I already made a concession," Sydney protested, "when I agreed to the carrels and the individualized programs. I wanted more interaction in the classroom, not less. Now you're pushing to control even their free time. I think you're losing the whole point of them being here."

"Tell him, Denise!" John slammed his hand down on the desk. He must have heard Sydney's veiled accusations about meddling fifty times or more. "They get plenty of time to interact after school hours. Didn't we promise Mrs. Shastri that we'd offer remedial work for slow ones, enrichment for the ones who are ahead?"

"I gave you the carrels, John, but this new thing of yours goes too far. It's meddling!"

John cringed.

"I say leave them alone." Sydney turned to Denise. "You agree with me, don't you, Denise?"

Denise flashed both palms at them. "Whoa. I haven't the faintest idea what you're talking about. Even if I did, I'm not going to be in the middle. I just came along for the ride."

"We're talking about Dennis Worchowski, the boy they call Demon. John says he's reading at about a third-grade level." Sydney slouched in his chair and pursed his lips.

Denise looked at John through questioning eyes.

"His math teacher noticed that Dennis always says he doesn't understand the instructions on his computer program." John smiled slyly at Denise. "He was very cleverly getting her to read them for him. She says the boy—"

"John wants to get one of the other students to tutor him. I say that would change something, some dynamic in the mix. We're at an impasse on this issue." Sydney took a deep breath. "Actually, Denise, we probably could use your help."

Mrs. McPhearson set the coffeepot and three cups on the credenza.

John poured and handed a cup to Denise. She signaled a no-thank-you to John's offer of cream and sugar.

"What if I agree with John, Syd?" She raised her eyebrow flirtatiously. "Will you still take me to Door County?"

"Maybe you could earn your keep." Sydney winked at her.

Denise laughed. "Wouldn't that make me a kept woman?"

John stifled a laugh. *How long has this little romance been going on?*

"Come on, Denise, let's get serious for a moment. John and I could use your help."

She winked at Sydney one last time before leaning forward in her chair. "OK, we'll get serious. I think you guys are arguing the wrong point. John, you say it won't upset things or change the dynamic; Syd, your point is that it would change things. Of course it would change things."

"There you have it." Sydney snapped his fingers. "Thank you, Denise."

"Slow down, Syd—you didn't let me finish. The question you should be debating is what's wrong with upsetting the mix? We've been around this block before with the twins issue."

Sydney started pacing about the room. "I conceded about the twins, but that was before the process actually started."

"You can't control everything, Syd!" John looked heavenward in his frustration with Syd's stubbornness.

Denise sighed. "Sit down, Syd. Listen to me. The process actually began long before they got here. We didn't exactly start with blank slates. In case you've forgotten, these kids were randomly selected from *one* social studies class. Besides, in the real world, people meddle. It can't be avoided."

"But that's just it!" Sydney sprang to his feet again. "I'm trying *not* to control, and this is *not* the real world. This is a scientific experiment. It should be kept in its own little cocoon if we're to get uncontaminated data."

"Sydney, get real. You can't possibly think these kids aren't being influenced by external dynamics. They're home right now talking to their parents, their pimps, and their dealers. There are certain natural circumstances that can't be avoided. Sit down, Sydney. You're making me nervous. If they were in a real school, the kid might get his tutor. You want real answers, don't you, Syd?" Denise turned to John. "Who'd you have in mind to do the tutoring?"

"Melissa Whistler." John quietly sipped his coffee. *Denise seems to know what's she's doing. Maybe she can get him to see reason.*

"Oh—I like that idea. How's Melissa been doing?"

"She does her assignments fine but spends all her free time in her room by herself."

"This plan of yours, it might be good for Melissa—draw her out of her shell a little."

John noticed Sydney sulking in the background as he answered, "I can't take all the credit. It was Wayne Beemers' idea. He said Melissa's done some tutoring before. She's good at it."

"I'll be darned!" Denise slapped her hand on her thigh. "There's more to that girl than I thought."

"Wayne says it's not good for her to be isolating herself in her room all the time, and I agree."

Denise turned her attention back to Sydney. "Yes, I can see what you mean, Syd. Assigning Melissa to tutor Dennis would be meddling."

Sydney sat forward in his chair. "I'm glad you've come to your senses, Denise. That settles it, then."

At first, John was encouraged by how expertly Denise seemed to be pleading his case. Now, he wasn't quite sure what direction she was going. He felt his muscles tense. *Looks like I could lose this round.*

Denise took Sydney's hand in hers and spoke softly. "You do want them to interact with each other, don't you, Syd?"

"Of course; that's the whole idea."

"Well then," John seized his opportunity, "let's get Melissa interacting."

"I still don't like it, assigning one student to interact with another…"

John was about to expand on his point about getting more interaction when he saw the warning look on Denise's face.

Denise was still holding Sydney's hand. "What if it was *their* idea, Syd? You want the kids to be in control—give them the information and let them decide for themselves."

"I still don't like it." Sydney's voice sounded hesitant.

"You have to admit, John's right on one count—Melissa's not doing much interacting now."

Sydney sighed. "I suppose it would get Melissa involved." He pulled his hand away from Denise's and shook his finger at John. "But don't you pressure them into doing something they don't really want to do."

Syd thinks I'm a meddler, but this gal's a master meddler. Thanks, Denise. "Trust me, Syd. I'll present the idea to them and let them make their own decisions about it."

"All right," Sydney conceded, "that's settled then. What's next?"

"I hope all this doesn't put a damper on your vacation plans."

Sydney spoke through clenched teeth. "You don't have anything else up your sleeve, do you, John?"

John wasn't eager to let Sydney in on what else was going on at the school. He pondered his response carefully before continuing his report. "The staff is just listening and taking notes, as per your instructions for now, Syd."

"For now? What do you mean, for now?"

"Bob Sweeney says the kids had themselves some big organizational meeting a couple of weeks ago. As it stands, they've lined themselves up into two camps. The girls' leader is Tashina Jones. The boys' is Karter Johnson."

Sydney frowned and slouched his shoulders. There was a downhearted edge of resignation in his voice. "I knew it. The bullies are taking over."

"To tell the truth, Syd, with those two running things, I'm more than a little concerned about some serious violence on the horizon—I'm afraid they might be needing that safety net we talked about…"

John shook his head sadly as he watched them drive off. *Denise, you've got yourself a tall order if you think you're going to loosen him up.*

Chapter Ten
Father John Meddles
December 1996

Melissa was surprised to see Mrs. Sweeney at her door with a message from Father John.

"What does he want?"

"Father didn't tell me what it's about." Mrs. Sweeney spoke through the crack in the door. "Only that he wants to see you in his office now."

Melissa had never been in a rectory before. The housekeeper showed her in, and Melissa wondered, *What's such a young woman doing with such an old man? Maybe she's his mistress.*

Regardless, she was glad for the presence of a woman in the house. Melissa didn't like to be alone with any man.

"Come in. Sit down, Melissa." Father John gestured toward the chair on the other side of his desk. "Would you like a glass of milk or a soft drink?"

"No thank you, sir." *I wonder if any of the others have been invited to private conferences with the good father.*

"I hear good things about you, Melissa. You're doing very well here. It's been noted that you're not only very intelligent, but a conscientious student as well."

He wants something. He didn't call me here to say I'm a good student. Get to the point, Father, she thought. She said merely, "Thank you."

"It's also been brought to my attention that you spend most of your free time alone."

Here it comes. The pitch. The lecture. You should spend more time with your peers, Melissa. Books are fine, but you need a social life too, Melissa. You're too serious, Melissa, you need to have some fun. Have you thought of joining a club, or perhaps learning to play an instrument and joining the band?

This time, she said, "I like being by myself, Father."

The concerned look she saw on Father John's face made Melissa feel anxious.

"Perhaps it's not good to be alone too much—I'll get right to the point, Melissa. I understand you've done some tutoring in reading. We have a student who could use the kind of help you could provide. Would you be interested in a tutoring assignment?"

Melissa took her time answering. *He's got to be talking about Maria Guliano or Demon Worchowski. They're the slower ones. Maria wouldn't be too bad, but Demon, that's a whole other story. One way or another, Father is going to make it hard for me to keep to myself. But at least there are worse things than tutoring.*

"I might consider it, Father."

"I'm glad to hear that, Melissa. I believe it would be a good arrangement for both of you."

"May I ask, Father, who are you talking about? Which student do you want me to tutor?"

"I'm not at liberty to say just yet. I have to check with the other student first. I'm not sure the other student will agree."

"Is that all, Father? Was there anything else you wanted to talk to me about?"

"No, that's it. You may be excused."

"Thank you, Father."

"Oh, and, Melissa, keep up the good work."

Melissa found her way out of the rectory. *Oh, let it be Maria. If there is a God, please let it be Maria.*

*****

Father John poked his head out the door at Demon Worchowski, who was sitting on the couch flipping through a *Catholic Herald.* "Hello, Dennis. Come in. Nice day today. I love how fresh and pure everything looks after a snowfall. Sit down. Would you like a soda or something?"

"Sure, thanks, Father. Do you have Pepsi?" Demon slid into the chair facing John's desk.

John called to Mrs. McPhearson to get the soft drink for Demon. "Oh, and bring one for me too, will you, please? Make mine a diet." He settled down in his plush office chair across from Demon, the desk between them.

"You're Catholic, aren't you, Dennis?"

"Yes, Father."

Mrs. McPhearson put the soft drinks on the desk.

"Thank you." John took a drink from his glass. "Ah, that's refreshing." He turned his attention back to the boy. "How is it that you haven't gone to one of our schools?"

"I did, Father, through the fifth grade." The boy relaxed in his seat. "Then I transferred to the public school. There're six of us. My parents can't afford the tuition all the way through."

"I see." *I guess we should be doing a better job with our own.* "School is hard for you, isn't it, Dennis?"

Demon took a drink from his paper cup and set in on the desk. "I do all right. It's just I ain't—I mean, I'm not much interested in school. I got other plans."

"Yes, I know, Dennis. You're looking forward to working in your father's construction business, is that right?"

"Yes, Father." Demon had a proud smile on his face. "I'm a good carpenter."

"As I understand it, Dennis, your father has some other ideas for you." John waited for the boy's response.

After a minute of fidgeting, Demon gave a heavy sigh. "Everything would've been just fine with my dad if I hadn't had the dumb luck to get picked for this experiment, or whatever you call it."

John rubbed his chin and took a moment before going on. "Has anyone ever suggested some remedial work for you, Dennis?"

"Yeah." Demon scowled. "They kept me back in fourth grade at St. Mary's. If they hadn't kept me back I'd be in high school now. I'd be playing football, and I sure wouldn't be in this mess."

"You know, Dennis," John responded quickly, automatically, without thinking—slipping into the role of priest, confessor, and counselor, "sometimes the Lord throws us a curve ball that we don't quite understand at the time. But there is wisdom in the Lord's plan. We need to trust in Him, persevere, and let Him guide us. Getting chosen for this program is part of God's plan for you, Dennis. There's a reason for everything, my boy."

Demon sighed and shook his head back and forth slowly. "If you say so, Father."

John looked straight into the boy's eyes. "You're in trouble, Dennis." His voice was soft. "I'd like to help you if you'll let me."

Demon bent his head down and fiddled with a button his shirt. "I don't know what you can do, Father." He looked up. "Unless you got some miracle up your sleeve."

"Well, the Lord works in strange ways. I just might have one." John gave the boy a reassuring smile.

"It's gonna take a whopper, Father."

"Listen to me, Dennis. I've been told that you're a smart enough young man, but you have three problems. One, you can't read. Two, you're very clever at hiding that fact, and three, you won't let anyone help you."

"I don't hafta read, Father." Demon's right leg jiggled up and down. "I'm already a better carpenter than most of the slugs my dad hires."

"I'll bet you are, Dennis. But your dad wants something more for you. He wants you to have options. Then if you choose the construction business, it'll be fine with him. If you and your friends—"

"I don't have any friends!" Demon's leg jiggled faster. "They all hate me!"

"Come on, Dennis." John kept his voice soft as he tried to soothe the boy. "They might be angry with you, but they don't hate you."

John listened sympathetically as Demon explained how Karter and Eddie had threatened him.

"They want you on their team, boy. They want the chance that the prize money can provide for them." John leaned forward. "You can't blame them for that. If you achieve Mr. Schuster's goals, you'll have the options your father wants for you. You can't blame him for wanting that for you either, Dennis. You owe it to him to at least try, don't you think?"

Demon squirmed.

"I believe that if you could just lick this reading problem, it wouldn't be so hard for you."

"You think I haven't tried?" Demon had a sour look on his face.

"Yes, but, unfortunately you haven't had much help. I think with some private tutoring and some very hard work, you could be reading at your grade level in just a few months."

Demon shook his head. "I don't know, Father."

"You got a better plan?"

"No, I guess not." Demon slouched down in the chair.

"Well, Dennis," John continued enthusiastically, "I've talked with Melissa Whistler, and she's agreed to work with you, to help you. Melissa's done some tutoring in the past. I understand she's very good at it."

Demon sprang from his chair trembling, screaming, and stomping his feet.

The shock of the boy's response rendered John momentarily catatonic. He stood stock-still as Demon bolted out of the room and through the front door.

As soon as he came to his senses, John ran after him, but there was no way he could keep up with the adrenaline-pumped body of an adolescent. He went back to the rectory and called the police.

John was still out of breath when he talked to the dispatcher. "There's a boy from our school here at St. Joan's Parish. He's upset. There's no telling what he might do. He's running east on Main Street toward the Five Corners. His name is Dennis, Dennis Worchowski, likes to be called Demon. Can you bring him back here to the rectory when you find him?"

"We're on it, Father."

John paced nervously for an hour before he got the call back from the police.

"Hello, Father Murphy. This is Officer Cameron. We have Dennis Worchowski safely in custody."

"Thank the Lord."

"We've called his parents; they're on their way. We think maybe you should come down here too—"

"I thought you'd bring him back here, to the rectory?"

"There seems to be an awful lot of explaining to do, Father…"

"I was just telling the boy about a plan for his tutoring, and suddenly he went into this fit. He started shaking—"

"Father, it would be best if you come to the station and do the explaining in person."

"Yes, of course, I can do that…"

John placed the receiver on the hook and took a very deep breath. *An out-of-control boy who just left the company of a priest, and immediately they jump to their dirty little conclusions. Hold your temper, John. Keep your head. It's the boy who's in trouble. It's not about you.*

John made the sign of the cross and said a short prayer before he drove himself to the police station.

He entered the harshly lit station house and addressed the dispatcher, who was staring intently at her computer behind the counter.

When he got her attention, he said, "Hello, I'm Father John Murphy. I'm here about the Worchowski boy. I believe you have him in custody?"

She raised one eyebrow as she peered up at him through wide eyes. "Yes, yes, of course. You're Father John, from St. Joan's. Have a seat, Father. Officer Cameron will be right with you." She punched some buttons on her keyboard.

It wasn't long before Officer Cameron came out and offered John his hand. John followed him to a cubicle behind the counter. "Sit down, Father." He gestured toward a small metal chair.

John looked around at the sterile environment. "Are you one of the officers who apprehended the boy?"

"Yes, I am."

"Could you please fill me in on what happened? I thought you'd bring him back to the rectory."

"It's a good thing you called us, Father. The boy was obviously pretty distraught. A kid running down the middle of the road with his arms flying in all directions wasn't hard to find. My partner flipped on the siren and blinked the lights, but the boy just kept running. Officer Clark stopped the squad car to let me out. The boy kicked and screamed; he even bit me before I subdued him and got him into the car. After a few minutes of heavy breathing, he finally found his voice. What he said was very disturbing: 'Leave me alone! Supposed to be sacred! How could you do it! You spoiled everything! I trusted you!' You can understand our concern, Father."

John wasn't sure whether the look on Officer Cameron's face was accusatory or apologetic. "Yes, of course, I can. You did the right thing, Officer."

"We have to wait until the boy's parents get here before we can continue our investigation. I'll have to ask you to take a seat in the outer office. It shouldn't be too long."

John felt the knot in his chest tighten as he waited for whatever would come next. Another thirty minutes passed before he saw Demon's parents escorted past the counter. He fidgeted and paced until, finally, he was invited to join the meeting with the officers and Demon's parents.

When John entered the room, he saw Demon pounding his fist on the table. "I hate it! They all know, and they're all laughing at me!"

John was quick to pick up on what was going on. He walked over to where the boy was sitting. "That's not true, Demon. You've got to believe me. I didn't tell Melissa it was you I wanted her to tutor." John looked to Demon's father.

"Look, Demon, maybe this tutoring thing isn't such a bad idea. Maybe your mother and I should have gotten you some help a long time ago."

"Yeah, right! Even if Father didn't tell Melissa, how can you keep something like that a secret?" He pounded the desk again. "Me meeting with her all the time like that, just the two of us. If they don't know she's tutoring me, they'll fill in the blanks with something else." Demon relaxed his fist. His shoulders drooped, and he began to sob. "Oh, what's the use—I ain't got no friends at that school anymore, anyway. I just want to go home."

"Demon, honey," his mother pleaded, "you know what will happen if you drop out of the program."

Demon stomped his foot. "Damn!" He stomped again. "I ain't no martyr!" He stomped a third time, tears streaming down his cheeks. "Dad, don't make me do this."

"Look, son, I'm sorry I got you into this mess. I should have listened to you, left well enough alone. I'd sure be proud to have you as a partner someday—I know I have no right to ask you this, son, but I'm gonna ask anyway." Dennis Sr.'s voice was gentle but insistent. "I want you to go back to that school and stick it out. I want you to accept that girl's offer to tutor you."

"Dad, you don't know what it's like." The boy turned his tear-streaked face up to his father's.

Dennis Sr. put his arm around his son. "Don't you see, Demon? If you let Melissa tutor you, it will send a message to your friends that you're one of them. You're with them, serious about wanting the prize money."

Father John cleared his throat. "It's no sin to have a reading problem, boy. But I don't think you could live with yourself if it turned out that you were the one who kept the rest from getting their chance." He looked to Dennis Sr. again.

Dennis Sr. waited until Demon had finished blowing his nose and wiping his eyes. "I promise that if, after all of this is over, you still don't want to go to college, we'll just give your portion of the prize money back to Mr. Schuster. But you've got to do your part here. For yourself and for your friends, and for me too, Demon."

"I guess I don't have much choice, do I?" Demon wiped his eyes and sniffled. "One thing though… Father, we don't have to tell anyone about all this—I mean, about what happened here tonight—do we?"

"You have my word, Demon."

"And we won't be having any more of those meetings in the rectory? You'll let me handle things my own way?"

"OK, Demon."

"And you'll let me be the one who talks to Melissa too, OK? I mean like it was my idea, like I decided by myself?"

"OK, Demon."

John had a flashback to the meeting with Karter Johnson's parents last summer. Mrs. Johnson's words rang in his ears. *"I simply cannot believe that a man of the cloth, such as yourself, would deny young people the spiritual guidance they so desperately need."* A private smile crossed his face. *OK, Demon, I'll try not to meddle—any more.*

*****

Melissa was making her usual fast exit after classes when she heard Demon's voice. "Hey, Melissa, wait up. Can I talk to you for a minute?" Demon fell into step beside her.

"What do you want to talk about?" She kept walking.

Demon blurted, "Father John said you'd tutor me in reading."

"Oh…" She stopped walking. *Just my luck,* she thought. "He asked if I'd be interested in doing some tutoring, but he didn't say with whom."

"Um, it's me. The who is me. Father said you'd be willing to give me some reading lessons." Demon shifted from one foot to the other as he talked.

"Look, Demon." She started walking again. "Are you sure you really want to do this? I mean, are they making you do it?"

He picked up the pace to keep up with her. "Nah, not really—well, sorta."

Melissa stopped and faced Demon. "What will your smart-aleck, tough-guy friends think, you being tutored by me?"

"You can leave that part to me. I can handle them."

Yeah, sure, Demon, you can handle them. Who's going to handle you? She looked him straight in the eyes and struggled to hide her disappointment that it was Demon, and not Maria, she was expected to tutor. "Demon, if I'm going to tutor you, you've got to level with me. Why do you want to do this?"

"OK, OK. I suppose you could say it's one of them cooperation things. See, I never thought I'd ever want to go to college or anything like that. I still don't think I wanna go. I ain't never been much for the book stuff. The rest of you guys, though, you think it's a big deal. Karter and Eddie, they don't think I'm being a team player." He looked down at his feet. "And then there's my dad; he's an all-right guy, I guess. He wants me to keep my options open. I guess he's got a point—anyway, what do you say, Melissa?"

Melissa took a moment before answering, "Do you really want my help, or do you just want to make a show of it for your friends?"

Demon didn't answer, and Melissa went on. "Why should I waste my time with you if you don't really want to read?"

"You're a smart girl, Melissa." Demon's face turned red. "If I had my way, I'd be back in the old school, getting by. Then nobody would get the prize."

"Why should I trust you, Demon?" Melissa sighed. "We'd be spending a lot of time alone together." She looked him in the eyes and asked, "How can I tell what's on your mind?"

"Look, Melissa, maybe I got a problem with reading, but I ain't stupid. There's lots of things you can learn that don't come in books." He bounced from one foot to the other and stammered, "It's not that you're not good-looking enough, but I ain't interested in making things worse for myself than they already are. I need your help, Melissa."

"Let me think about it for a while. I'll give you my answer tomorrow."

"Sounds fair enough to me. Meet you here after class?" A friendly smile crossed Demon's face.

Melissa wasn't in a mood to smile. "Sure."

Melissa gave some serious thought to her options. The next day, she waited for Demon after class. "I'll do it, Demon—on one condition. If we're going to spend a lot of time together, you're going to have to concentrate on reading."

Demon shrugged his shoulders. "I suppose. Yeah, OK, Melissa. I'll try."

Chapter Eleven
Tensions Mount
January 1997

"Let's go find the little chocolate girl." Karter slurred his words as he and Eddie stumbled down the street past the Kwik-Mart.

"Nah, it's not worth the trouble. Too big a risk," Eddie mumbled.

"We ain't at school now. What we do here don't count for nothin. Whaddya say, Eddie? Let's go."

"I don't feel so good, Karter. Think I better go home and sleep off the gin. You're on your own."

"Yeah, Eddie, you do that," Karter shouted after him. "Who needs you anyway?" He hurled the empty bottle in the street.

Karter listed to one side as he walked away. *I'm gonna go get me some chocolate for dessert.* He walked the streets past Tashina's house, past the crack house and the darkened window of the storefront church next door. He checked out the George Webb all-night restaurant, where Tashina's grandmother worked. He searched the streets for about half an hour before he caught sight of her about a block ahead of him. *There she is, and she's by herself. Yes!* He ran to catch up and stumbled into step beside her. "Hey, Chocolate, want some?"

Karter hadn't even finished snickering when Tashina pulled her knife and thrust it into his ribs.

"I warned ya! Don't mess wit me, white boy! I tol ya I gives back twice what I gets." Tashina glared at Karter, the knife with his blood still in her hand.

Karter looked first at his bloody jacket, then at Tashina. His thoughts were fuzzy, and his vision blurred. He stammered, "Just a lil friendly gesture, Tashina. That's all."

"Any more a your 'friendly gestures,' Karter Johnson, and ya better be scared to sleep in your own bed at night. Ya better sleep wit your eyes open. I'm done wit you now, boy. I gives ya back twice. Ya come at me again, and it's revenge time. Now get! Get outta my sight!" She turned on her heels and headed down the street.

Karter watched until his image of Tashina got small and disappeared. *She coulda just told me to bug off. She didn't hafta pull no knife. I wouldn't a hurt her.*

He sat on the curb and put his hand inside his jacket. The blood from his wound felt sticky on his fingers. When he saw his bloody hand, he stood up and yelled to the wind, "She stabbed me!"

The more he thought about it, the angrier he got. He checked again to see if he really was bleeding. He realized the wound was only surface, but a perfectly good jacket was ripped and bloodied. *Next time I catch that little smart-ass girl on the streets by herself, she ain't gonna be so lucky. I won't be by myself, either. I'll show her not to mess with Karter Johnson.* He kicked at a beer can someone had thrown on the street and punched at the door of the storefront church. *I got connections. She's talkin revenge; I'll show her revenge.* He stopped and checked again. At the sight of his own blood, he vowed, "You give me twice, I give you three times—four!"

*****

Tashina tossed around restlessly in her bed. She kicked the covers off and retrieved them. She got up and went to the bathroom for a glass of water. When she'd finished drinking, she slammed the glass down hard on the sink.

"That you, honey?" Her mother's voice came from the other bedroom.

"It's me, Mama." *Mama alla time like a good story.* "Jus gettin some water, Mama." *Think I be keepin this one to myself.*

"Good night, honey."

"Good night, Mama."

Damn that Karter! He could get me kicked outta the program. Course he'd get his butt kicked out, too. She peered at her image in the mirror. *Use you head, girl. He ain't dat stupid.*

Tashina went back to her room and closed the door. She made a fist with one hand and paced as she jabbed at the palm of her other hand. *He gots dat big plan a his. We don't hafta get along.* She lay down on her bed and punched at her pillow. *We don't hafta like each other.* She punched again. *We jus hafta make it look good.* She gave her pillow one more hard punch and turned off the light. *We don't hafta like each other. I hope you right bout dat one, Karter Johnson.*

Back at school, Tashina felt like she had the upper hand with Karter. Instead of engaging with him in their usual banter, she scowled at him at every opportunity. She talked Becca into having some fun at Karter's expense.

Maria was waiting for Moe in the living room, a little early for their usual meeting time, when Karter sneaked up behind her and poked her in the ribs.

Tashina and Becca, who'd been hiding behind the couch, leaped out at him and yelled, "Gotcha!"

Karter jumped back, did an about-face, put his hands in his pockets, and tramped off without a word. He didn't look back either. Maria just stood there looking stunned.

"See dat? Did ya see dat, Becca? Karter Johnson turnin whiter than Pepsodent." Tashina poked Becca on the arm and doubled over with laughter.

"Did you see the look on his face when we jumped out at him? We sure scared him, Tashina."

"Whooo-eee, I'm bettin he jus peed his pants."

Tashina, still laughing, looked at Maria and waved her finger. "You jus got yourself a lesson in girl power, girl. Free a charge."

Tashina and Becca were slapping their thighs and laughing so hard the tears came to their eyes.

When the laughing twosome shared their adventure with Jenna, Jenna didn't see the humor. "You got lucky," she said. "If Eddie or Sam had been there—maybe even Demon—you'd have had more trouble than you bargained for. When are the two of you *girls* going to learn to engage your brains before you activate your mouths and your fists?"

"Yeah, OK, Jenna, we got the point." Becca rolled her eyes at Tashina.

"Yeah, me and Becca gots it. We try to be more careful in the future." Tashina winked at Becca. The two of them choked back another laugh and settled down to homework and gossip.

"Maria tol me Moe already got a wife picked for him." Tashina slapped her thigh. "She two years old. Can ya believe it! A two-year-old bride."

"Jews used to do that." Jenna closed her book and looked at Tashina. "Some still do."

"Nah, you kiddin me."

"The *shatkin* made the arrangements." Becca smirked at Tashina.

Jenna explained, "A *shatkin* is usually a yenta—a nosy old gossip, but that's part of her job. She needs to know things about people—"

"If she's going to be able to make matches that will be accepted," Becca finished her sister's thought.

Tashina felt like she was watching a tennis match.

Becca laughed. "Maybe the yenta would pick Karter for you, Tashina."

"Nobody picks nobody for dis girl!" Tashina spat out her angry words. "If there's ever gonna be any pickin for dis girl, she gonna be the one doin the pickin!"

Jenna sighed. "Well, nobody's going to do any picking for Becca and me, either. We don't have a dowry."

Tashina's eyes got wide. "What's at?"

"The money the bride's father gives to the boy that marries her." Jenna went on in a somber voice, "Our father doesn't have enough money to take care of his new family, let alone take care of his first family—us and Ralph, that is."

"I don't get it. The father pay the guy to marry his daughter?" Tashina slapped her forehead with the palm of her hand. "She can't get no good-for-nothin man on her own merits? Now I *knows* I heard it all."

"If we get that prize money, we won't need a dowry or a man, and that's fine with me." Becca cleared her throat. "I haven't seen one yet that I'd want to hook up with…. Think we'll get it—the money?"

"Not if you two don't learn to control your fists and your mouths." Jenna glared at Tashina. "What happened between you and Karter?"

"Ain't none a you business. Jus leave his white ass to me." Tashina gave Jenna a chilly stare.

"OK, OK. Just be careful, Tashina."

*****

Karter, Eddie, and Sam had sneaked off to town again to talk to some local girls.

Karter set the pace, as usual. "What do you guys think about Buddy Boy and the quiet one?"

"I don't know." Sam kicked a stone as they walked. "I think Demon's on the up and up. He told us straight out that Melissa was tutoring him—said maybe he changed his mind about the college thing."

"Just the same, I'm keeping my eye on him." Karter snarled.

Eddie stopped. "Hey, you guys, got any cash on you?"

Karter and Sam turned around to face him. Karter raised his eyebrows. "What kinda cash you talking about, Eddie?"

"I met this girl in town, says she can put us on to some good grass."

Karter punched Eddie in the shoulder. "Hey, nice work, Eddie. That ought to make this trip worth our efforts."

The three pooled their cash and decided that between them they ought to be able to get a bag. They picked up the pace as they continued on their journey.

"What about that sly fox, Moe? Bet he's getting some." Karter sniggered. "Didn't I tell you? Didn't I tell you guys? I told you guys she'd like the attention."

Sam shrugged. "Yeah, Karter, you told us."

Karter passed the other two. He turned around and walked backwards, facing them. "She likes it. I know one when I see one." Karter grinned. "Didn't I peg her right?"

Eddie picked up a stone from the road and tossed it to Karter. "Yeah, Karter. It's Moe you didn't figure."

"You got me on that one, Eddie."

Karter turned around and let the others catch up. They walked three abreast without talking until Karter broke the silence. "What's she see in him anyway? He's such a little guy—I bet his pecker's not much bigger than a baby dill."

With that, they all howled and jabbed each other's shoulders until they were out of breath and practically rolling on the ground.

When Sam caught his breath, he sighed. "Yeah, well, Moe's a nice guy. Sometimes, nice guys get them. Girls, especially the shy ones like Maria, they probably like the little guys—the warm, sensitive types." He laughed. "Hey man, you guys might learn a thing or two from Moe." He poked Eddie in the arm and clipped Karter's shoulder. "I don't see you getting any."

They all laughed good-naturedly.

"Speaking of getting any," Eddie risked a question, "what's going on between you and Tashina, Karter? She sure is on your case."

Karter swung around and clipped Eddie in the mouth. "Ain't none a your business!"

Eddie wiped the blood from his lip on his sleeve. "I was just asking, Karter."

Karter stood glaring at Eddie with his fist in midair. Then he turned around and headed back toward the school. He shouted at them over his shoulder. "Why can't people just mind their own damn business!"

Eddie and Sam shrugged their shoulders at each other and continued toward town.

*****

Chapter Eleven

Melissa, as usual, was eating her supper quietly as she watched and listened. There was always something to learn from her classmates, especially if she didn't join the conversation.

"Anyone interested in a little partying should congregate in the schoolyard after dark," Eddie said in a stage whisper. There was nothing ambiguous about his meaning.

Becca slammed her fork on the table. "Look, Eddie! What you do on your own time on the weekends is your business, but Schuster's rules are clear. Are you sure you want to jeopardize all of our chances by taking the risk you're talking about?"

"Geez, Becca. All I'm talking about here is a little friendly sharing. I could have just kept it all for myself." He pounded his fist on the table. "You're so damned all the time uptight. Ain't we supposed to be trying to be friends here?" He stormed out of the room.

The next day, Melissa was in the kitchen fixing herself a snack when she noticed Becca approach Eddie in the dining room. She stopped what she was doing and stood perfectly still.

"How're you doing, Eddie?" Becca said. Just like that.

Eddie looked to his left and then to his right. "You talking to me?" Melissa ducked behind the door just in time to avoid being seen.

Becca's voice sounded friendly. "Yeah. I was hoping to get your opinion."

Melissa risked another peek, and she saw Eddie pointing at his chest. "You want *my* opinion?" he asked.

Becca answered, "Yeah. Do you know what's going on with Karter?"

Melissa hid behind the door again. Her skin felt prickly. *I think he saw me.* From then on, she listened from out of sight. Eddie's voice was the next one she heard.

"Damned if I know. Karter's been acting weird about stuff lately. He's scary, man. Sometimes he acts like he's gonna explode or something. The next thing you know, he's all quiet and sulky. Something must have happened over Christmas break because he ain't been the same since. I don't know what the hell's going on around here. Nobody's acting like their normal self."

Becca sounded worried. "I can't figure it out either, Tashina won't talk about it. The mere mention of Karter's name and she clams up—I think you're right, Eddie. Something must have happened between her and Karter."

"Karter's not talking about it, that's for sure. If he was gonna tell somebody, it'd be me."

"I've been thinking—maybe we should have another meeting. We still have to figure out a plan for us to get the prize money, but I'm worried about what might happen with Karter and Tashina in the same room and no teacher there to keep the peace. What do you think, Eddie?"

Melissa waited until Eddie and Becca finished their conversation and left the dining room to take the sandwich she'd prepared to her room. As she passed Becca in the hall, she smiled and said, "Hi."

Becca answered, "Hi, Melissa," as she glanced at the sandwich with a puzzled expression on her face.

Chapter Eleven

Melissa didn't offer any explanations.

*****

During dinner one night, Karter was sitting peaceably enough. He wasn't asking for trouble. But when Becca spilled some catsup on his pants, he jumped to his feet and gave her the finger. He screamed. "What the F is matter with you? I ought to just dump the whole bottle on you, see how the hell you like it!" He brushed at his pants with his napkin.

Heads stayed down until Becca yelled back at him, just as loud, "It was an accident. Deal with it!"

Karter sat down. "All right, all right, I got the message, Becca."

Karter saw Tashina smirking at him. He picked up his fork and made angry stabs at his food. The students consumed the remainder of their meal in silence.

*****

Melissa looked at the clock—9:30. She was done with her homework and she couldn't resist cracking the door open to eavesdrop on her classmates. As usual, there was something to be learned. This time, she watched as Sam met Moe coming out of Maria's room. Moe looked glum.

"Hey Moe, what's up? Woman trouble?"

Moe snapped back, "Shut your dirty mouth! What is between Maria and me is not any of your business."

"Hey man, I thought we were friends. Friends get worried about each other sometimes."

Moe frowned and slouched his shoulders. "I didn't mean anything about you, Sam. I have some things—some private things—to work out in my own head."

"I was just trying to help."

"Sometimes it is better for friends to back away."

Sam put his hand up for a half-hearted high-five. "I get the message," he said, and the two walked toward their separate rooms.

*****

When the weekend rolled around, ten students boarded the bus to go home. It was a quiet ride.

Chapter Twelve
Weekend at Home
February 1997

Maria cupped her hand over the mouthpiece of the telephone. "No." She looked around to see if anyone was in earshot. "No news."

She listened to Moe's despondent voice. "I am very sorry, Maria."

"I know. Me too…"

"We will figure something out," Moe whispered.

"Yeah, sure." Maria stretched the phone cord from the hall to the kitchen and looked to see if anyone was there. "Did you tell anyone?"

"I have talked with my brother about it. Jahan is a year younger than I am, but sometimes I think he is the older one. He scolded me for not taking the precautions."

"You shouldn't have told," Maria whispered into the phone.

"I have certainly made a mess of things. Not any of us will get the college money now."

"We don't know for sure, yet."

"I would not ask you this on my own, Maria. I promised my brother I would ask you if you would consider abortion."

"That would be a sin." Maria was quiet for a moment. "I'm glad it's not you that's asking, Moe."

"It is not me that I am concerned about. I am a useless failure. The world would be better off without my presence in it."

"Don't talk like that, Moe."

"I promised Jahan I would not do anything drastic, but I can think of at least one or two others who would do it for me whether I want them to or not."

Maria saw her father coming toward the kitchen. "Where's your mother, Maria?"

"I'm on the phone, Dad." She yelled into the mouthpiece, "I gotta go now, Tashina."

Moe said, "Maybe we will get lucky."

"Yeah, maybe," she whispered.

*****

Karter whispered. "She's dark chocolate, the real bittersweet kind." Rick was driving. Karter was in the front passenger seat and two other boys were in the back of the ancient Chevy that Rick's dad managed to keep running.

"See, she plays it this way. At first she acts like she don't want it, talks real sassy-like. Don't let that fool you. She wants it, man—she wants it real bad."

Karter knew he had Rick's attention when he saw the lust in Rick's eyes and the smirk on his face. "But she wants to know you want it bad; you gotta want it real bad too, and she's gonna make you work for it. I'll tell you, man, it's worth it."

Rick kept his eyes on the road without a word. Karter snorted. *Oh, he's hooked all right. I can practically see his pants pointing.* "You gonna have hot chocolate all over your lily-white body, just a-screamin and a-hollerin and lovin it, lovin it all. I don't know if you can handle it, man—you'll probably come in your own pants before you can even give her what she wants."

"You let me worry about that," Rick snapped back at him.

When Karter saw Tashina walking toward the George Webb, he told Rick to pull over and park the car. Tashina was already inside the restaurant—out of their sight—when the boys got out of the car to wait on the street. They were high on pot and all hyped up.

About ten minutes later, Tashina left the restaurant laughing. "Bye, Grams. Thanks for treatin my friends special," she yelled over her shoulder as she passed through the door.

Karter's face was the color of whiteout over a misspelled word when he saw that Maria was with Tashina.

Rick whirled around and looked at Karter. "You set me up to hit on Tashina!" The spit flew out of Rick's mouth and smacked Karter in the face. "What kinda fool you think I am? He turned and grabbed Karter by the collar and shouted, "You were gonna hit on my sister while I was busy with Tashina! You stupid little S.O.B.! You ain't fit to wipe the butt of the likes of Tashina Jones. I'm gonna kill you!"

Rick hit hard, and Karter went down. Rick jumped on top of him and began punching him in the face. Karter heard Tashina yelling, "Get off him, Rick. He ain't worth it! Stupid little virgin boy's all talk. Get off him! He ain't done nothin but talk."

Karter scrambled to his feet. Rick grabbed him by the collar with one hand and slapped his face with the other. Tashina jumped on Rick's back and held on tight. Maria grabbed hold and pulled at her brother's jacket. Still, Rick held his grip on Karter. Rick hit Karter in the face several more times before Tashina screamed in his ear at the top of her powerful lungs. "Let him go, Rick!"

Rick let Karter fall to the ground. Karter lay there looking up at Rick and groaning. "Don't hit me no more, Rick. I'm hurt bad," he pleaded. Rick gave him one hard kick in the groin before he turned to Tashina. "You're right, Tashina. He ain't worth it."

Rick and the two other boys headed for the car. Rick nodded toward Tashina and Maria. "They can handle it," he said to his friends.

Karter felt Tashina's onion breath on his face as she knelt over him. "You OK, Karter? You gonna be needin some medical tention here? Should I be callin a doctor or somethin?"

Karter made a feeble attempt to get to his feet, groaned, and slumped back to the ground. His nose was bleeding. "Nah, think I'm gonna be all right. I guess I owe you, Tashina."

Tashina stood over him with her hands on her hips. "Ya owes me all right, Karter Johnson. Ya owes me an apology. Maria here could stand to get one too. Ya gotta learn to treat people wit respec! Ya gets what ya dish out, and the quicker you learns dat, Karter Johnson, the better for alla us." She pulled a tissue from her pocket, knelt over Karter again and dabbed at his nose with the tissue.

"Ouch." He pushed Tashina's hand away. "I said I owe you, Tashina. Could you just please go now and leave me alone? Just leave me the God-damned hell alone."

"Ya sure you OK? I mean ya don't need me to be callin no doctor or nothin?"

"I'm fine, Tashina. Just go! Leave me alone."

*****

On Sunday morning, Tashina waited outside St. Jude's for Maria. The girls walked together in silence for several blocks before Maria spoke.

"You know, me and Moe, we've been real close over these past few months."

"Yeah, I noticed. Didn't I tell ya you was playin wit fire? How come ya don't never listen to me? He knocked ya up, didn't he?"

"Tashina, it's not like that. We were stupid. It's not just his fault. I was willing. We were both stupid."

195

"Damn! I was right den." Tashina stomped her feet, first one, then the other, then again she stomped with arms waving and hands flying in the air. "Damn! You pregnant! How far along ya?"

"I'm two weeks late—"

"Then ya don't know for sure."

"—for my second period."

Tashina's eyes narrowed. She grabbed Maria by the shoulders. "It ain't too late. Hear me, girl? We gonna talk to my mama. She gots connections. Nobody needs to know. I'm glad ya tol me fore it gots too late."

"I can't do that," Maria's voice was a whisper.

"Ya keepin it? Ya can't do dat! Don't ya know, girl, you messin wit the lives a nine other people? Mine is one a dem. Schuster's rules was clear bout dat subjec: Nobody gets pregnant!"

"We could get married."

Tashina screeched at her. "Ya some kinda crazy, girl? You fourteen. How old's he? He look like he eleven. It don't work dat way."

Maria had tears in her eyes. "We love each other, Tashina."

"Dat don't cut nothin. Ya think Mr. Schuster is gonna adopt ya—and Moe—and your kid? Wise up, little white girl; it don't work dat way." Tashina smacked her forehead with the palm of her hand. "He may be jus dyin to give his money away, but jus like alla us, he want somethin back for it! What'd he want wit your kid, anyway?"

"You're right, Tashina," Maria shouted. "I should have listened. I should have listened to my pastor. I should have listened to my parents. I should have listened to my teachers. I should have listened to my Lord. I should have listened to the Blessed Virgin. And I should have listened to you too, Tashina. I should have listened." Maria was breathing hard.

The two girls stood facing one another.

"Now what am I going to do? I don't need any lectures. I need a friend. I don't know what I need. Help me, Tashina. Help me figure out what to do."

Tashina shook her head. "I don't know what I gonna do wit ya, girl. Who else ya tell?"

"I didn't tell anyone, Tashina—only you," Maria sobbed.

"I gots ta get my head on for dis one. Don't ya tell nobody. They find out soon enough. Hear me, girl, keep dat mouth a yours shut til Tashina here figures somethin out."

"Moe told his brother."

Tashina slapped herself on the forehead again. "Ya sure picked a good one, Maria. Tell dat boy, from now on, he keep dat mouth a his shut. He better keep dat zipper a his shut too. Maybe you ain't pregnant—yet. Hear me, girl?"

Chapter Thirteen
Denise Confesses
Chicago, March 1997

Sydney was elated when Denise called and asked if she could come to see him. He'd given up on any hope of a continuing relationship with her. The weekend in Door County had been a disaster. He hadn't seen her since.

"I hope you don't mind having lunch in, Denise." He took her coat and hung it in the closet. "Kevin's an excellent cook.

"Kevin seems to be a man of many talents."

Sydney beamed with admiration as he watched her gracefully move toward the window. "He's made cucumber soup, moussaka, and his own special pastries for dessert."

"Mmmm, sounds good. The lake makes for an impressive view, even in March." She turned to face him, an inviting smile on her face. "I can't think of a more lovely place to have lunch than in an enchanting penthouse with a handsome prince. I feel like a princess."

Sydney arranged the flowers in the vase on the table, pulled the chair out for her, and poured the wine. "You said you had something important to tell me, something that might affect the project?"

Denise settled into the chair Sydney held out for her. "It's about one of the students—the one that's been tutoring the Worchowski boy, Melissa Whistler. I'm not sure how John got them to agree to do it, but it seems to be working OK. At least that's what I hear from Melissa."

Sydney poured the wine and seated himself. "How come you're talking to Melissa? I thought we decided you weren't going to get mixed up in the project?"

"Yeah, I know. That was the plan, Syd." Denise raised her glass of wine as if to make a toast. "But like it or not, I'm in it now."

Sydney felt the knot tighten in his stomach. "Don't get me wrong, Denise, it's always good to see you under any circumstances. But why is it that you and John don't call meetings to tell me good news?"

"You haven't called me either, Syd—not since Door County…"

Sydney flinched. "I didn't think you wanted me to. I wasn't much fun."

"It's always good to see you under any circumstances, Syd."

Sydney raised his glass. "Touché." He laughed. "OK, let's get on with it. How did you get mixed up in this thing?"

Denise tapped her fingers on the table. "One Friday night last December, Melissa showed up on my doorstep.

How in the world she found me and why she picked me, I don't know. I mean, I am in the book—not that hard to find. What I don't quite get is why she chose me."

"What are you saying, Denise? Don't tell me the girl is living with you?"

"I guess you could say that."

"No?" Sydney's mouth dropped open.

"I know it's stupid of me. I know I'm taking some major risks here—"

"It certainly would seem that way."

"She's just the kind of thing I've been avoiding for the past five years, ever since those boys tried to steal my purse on the school parking lot—and here I am in over my head again…"

She got up and walked to the window. "I vowed I'd never let myself care about them, never let myself be vulnerable, but I couldn't just turn her away. Back to the streets, girl, off with you! I just couldn't do it." Her voice trailed off.

Sydney stood behind her and spoke softly. "Hold on a moment, Denise. This sounds like serious business. I want to hear the whole story." He called to Kevin. "Could you please postpone lunch for a little while?"

"Certainly, sir. Let me know when you're ready." Kevin placed the ice bucket with the wine bottle and the glasses on the glass-top table between the two swivel chairs in front of the window.

They sat down and turned their chairs to face each other. Sydney reassured Denise with a smile. "Go on, I'm listening."

"She's really not much trouble. She reads a lot, and she can be good company."

"Hmm." Sydney nodded for her to go on.

"That first night, I called her mother. The woman was incoherent. There was some commotion happening in the background, and I couldn't make out what was going on. All that came through was, 'Yeah, sure, Lady. You just take care of my little girl.' I don't think she even knew who I was."

Sydney shook his head. "How can parents be so irresponsible? I just don't get it."

"Melissa told me her mother's boyfriend was stalking her, Syd…"

"Poor kid."

"Even her older brother scares her. The kid was staying out as much as she could. She waited until everyone in the house was too stoned or drunk to notice her slip in. Then she got up and out before they woke up. Spent her days in the library downtown, just to get out of the cold. It's obvious her mother knows what's going on—"

"I thought you said her mother didn't even care to know where the girl was."

"Her mother left money on the kitchen table for her, for a bus and McDonald's. Maybe that was the best she could do. Melissa just stayed as far away as she could for as long as she could." Denise reached for her wine and shook her head. "I just couldn't turn her out."

"What about Child Protection Services? Did you try calling them?"

Chapter Thirteen

"I suppose that's what I would have done if she'd come to me at school. I'd have been able to keep my boundaries—but she was on my doorstep! She just stood there and asked, 'Can I come in?' I said, 'Melissa. Melissa Whistler. What are you doing here?' She just asked again, 'Can I come in?' Well, I couldn't say no—she was freezing half to death, for Christ's sake!"

Sydney was taken back by Denise's defensive attitude. "Yes, but after—I mean after you let her in and got her warmed up, perhaps gave her something to eat, didn't you call the authorities? She was a runaway, Denise—you know better."

"Yes, I know better—I know too much!" She slapped her hand on the coffee table. "Child Protective Services is overwhelmed with too many cases and too few workers. Some of the most serious crap slips through the cracks!"

Sydney wasn't surprised at Denise's anger at the system. Still, he didn't know how to react, how to be helpful.

"It's funny," Denise went on, "and I don't mean funny like in ha-ha. We're required by law to report incidences of abuse, but reporting them turns out to be an exercise in futility—we know nothing much will happen. Sometimes blowing the whistle makes matters worse for the victims." She sighed. "But you can bet your booties we cover our butts and we report."

Sydney shook his head and smiled indulgently. "Still you took a risk, Denise. You didn't cover your butt very well this time."

"I did call her mother, Syd. Give me a little credit here."

"Still…"

"Even if the system did take Melissa on, she'd end up in some group home run by well-meaning but inexperienced young optimists. She probably wouldn't stay in a place like that for very long, anyway. No privacy, no place to hide. Or she could end up in some foster home with a bunch of other troubled kids…. Finding a placement? That could take weeks, even months. What's she supposed to do in the meantime? Live on the streets?"

Sydney was touched by Denise's fierce commitment to the girl. *She'd like people to think she's a lot tougher than she is.* "God, Denise, I don't know what to say." He reached for her hand.

"I did get in touch with her social worker that Monday. And I've applied for my foster care license. At least for the time being, I'm a port in the storm for her."

"Sounds to me more like you're in for the long haul." Sydney hesitated. "But a sixty-year-old woman raising a thirteen-year-old kid? Are you sure you're up for that kind of hassle?"

Denise squeezed Sydney's hand. "I might be in for the biggest let-down of my life, Syd, but I've decided to risk it."

Sydney squeezed her hand back. "OK, Denise, I think I understand. Does John know?"

"Not yet, but I don't see how Melissa's weekend residence should be any concern of his. I'm not asking permission, Syd; I'm just informing."

"Nobody's trying to talk you out of anything, Denise." He let loose of her hand and reached for his wine. "Not that it should have affected your decision, but if you had thrown her to the system, she'd be out of the project. What about the other students? Do they know?"

"I don't know what Melissa's told them. I doubt she's told them anything. When she decides to close up, she's one tough clam to open." Denise shook her head. "Since that first weekend, she hasn't talked about her family. To my knowledge, she's not contacted them either. She does have a social worker though, so I guess she talks to her—as much as she has to, that is."

"Hmm. I guess it's her business."

"Yeah, I guess."

"You know, if this character is as bad as you think, and he's out after her, what's to stop him from looking for her at your house? You could be in danger."

"I think that would be pretty remote."

"I'm worried about you, Denise."

"He could come looking for her in the Falls too, you know."

"Still…"

"The bus drops her off at my school along with the others on Friday nights. She waits 'til they're gone, and then she comes to my office and we ride home together. Same kind of routine on Monday mornings. I suppose if he were going to make a move on her, that's where it would happen. Melissa doesn't know it, but I've alerted the cop on the beat to keep an eye out for her."

Sydney was silent for a moment. *I like this softer side of her. She looks so vulnerable.*

Denise interrupted his thoughts, "So what are you thinking? Am I nuts or what?"

"You're a very nice person, Denise. Don't try so hard to hide it. You're much more attractive when you let it show."

Chapter Fourteen
Karter's Plan
March 1997

Secrets, like babies, have to be pushed out eventually. *It gotta be tol. But who gonna do the tellin and to who? And what gonna happen when it be tol?*

Tashina sat at the dinner table with her classmates. She heard the scraping of forks on plates and an occasional cough. What she didn't hear was the usual chatter. *They all knows somethins up.*

Maria sat with her elbows on the table and her head in her hands. *She so dumb bout how it is—she only know how it sposed to be.*

Moe, in his usual place next to Maria, studied his plate with his hands in his lap. Tashina poked at her cold potatoes and shook her head. *The three a us, we gots ourselves a secret all right.*

She scanned the other muted diners. Karter, who usually insisted on being the center of attention, shoveled down meatloaf and mashed potatoes, seemingly oblivious to the drama. *I wonder how he gonna take the news,* she pondered as her eyes moved on.

Jenna and Becca were silently gawking at each other as they absentmindedly raised forks from plates to mouths and back again. Melissa was fidgeting with her napkin. Demon's foot was jiggling faster than usual. Sam, ordinarily the first to grab seconds of any meal, was picking at his food. Eddie was alternately tapping his fingers on the table and peering at Maria.

Tashina had more on her plate than she could manage, and she didn't have much time to figure it out.

The stark inertia of the room was abruptly interrupted when Maria jumped out of her chair and screamed, "What are you all looking at me for? What am I—some kind of freak? Stop! Stop it! Stop staring at me!"

No one moved, chewed, or scraped a fork on a plate. The sound of Maria's screeching voice echoed in Tashina's ears. It was as if the movie had stopped and waited for her to do something—anything.

After what seemed like an eternity of a collectively held breath, Tashina got up and moved with determination. She fired a look that defied her classmates to interfere and went to comfort her friend.

She put an arm around the trembling girl's shoulder. "C'mon, Maria, it be OK. C'mon, girl."

Maria pushed Tashina's arm away. "You all hate me, don't you? Just say it," she screamed. "'I hate you, Maria Guliano.' You're thinking it." Her eyes were wild and frantic as they darted around the room. "Just say it! Say it!"

Tashina saw the door from the kitchen open a crack. She was relieved to know the Sweeneys were there, just in case things got nasty.

The rest stayed obediently in their seats until Tashina finally managed to escort the hysterical mother-to-be to her room. They closed the door, and Maria sobbed in Tashina's arms like a baby herself.

"They all hate me. They want me to kill my baby."

"Ain't nobody gonna hurt ya, girl. I tol you, stick by me. They ain't gonna mess wit Tashina here. You safe wit me."

Tashina continued to rock the sobbing girl and rub her back. *She done a real dumb thing here, but she don't deserve to die for it.... No tellin what might happen if Karter's rage kick in—I could handle him, but he gots Eddie wit him—maybe Sam and Demon too. Who I got? Maybe Becca, dat's all. Gotta do somethin. Can't leave her alone.*

Tashina took a tissue from the box and handed it to Maria. "Ya stay here. Lock the door after me. I'm gonna go get Melissa. Don't let nobody in but me. Hear me, girl?"

Maria blew her nose. "OK. Whatever you say, Tashina."

Tashina closed the door softly behind her. She knocked on Melissa's door and wasn't surprised when Melissa opened it only enough to see one eye.

"What do you want, Tashina?"

"I needs you help. Trust me; ask questions later," she whispered through the crack in the door.

Tashina kept her hope up even though Melissa held a firm grip on the door.

"What do you want me to do?"

"We can't talk here in the hall. Come to Maria's room."

Maria unlocked the door, let them in, and immediately resumed her fetal position on the bed.

"I want ya to stay wit her, Melissa. Lock the door after me, and don't let nobody in til I gets back."

"What's going on here, Tashina? Is she sick?"

"I ain't got time to talk now. Jus do what I say."

"But—"

"Dis here's a crisis!" Tashina gave Melissa the stoniest look she could muster. "Do what I say."

Tashina shut the door and waited to hear Melissa lock it after her before she went to Becca's room.

Once Tashina was inside with the door closed, Becca and Jenna guessed at what happened.

Becca gasped and put her hand over her mouth. "Did Karter rape her?"

"No, but I think he gonna kill her when he hears."

Becca shook her head. "If it wasn't Karter—"

"—it must be Moe, then," Jenna finished the sentence.

"Yeah. It wasn't no rape, neither."

"Oh my God! She's pregnant!"

Tashina nodded.

Becca's eyes were as big and round as twin full moons on a cloudless night. "What do you think Karter's going to do to them?

Tashina shrugged her shoulders and looked at the ceiling. "Damned if I knows."

"How far along is she?"

"Bout ten weeks."

"Thank God it's not too late." Becca moved to hug Tashina.

Tashina backed off. "Don't get you hopes up. She ain't bout to do dat. We already had dat little discussion."

"I guess that's it then; it's over." Becca flopped down on the bed.

Jenna grabbed her coat. "Yeah, I guess. We need help. We better tell Father John. Let's go."

"Hold on. There's one more thing we gots to do first. Maria be locked in the room wit Melissa. She be safe til we gets to Father John. But much as I hates to save his sorry ass, we gotta be sure Moe someplace safe fore we goes." Tashina looked around the room. "You gots a coat I can wear? I didn't stop to get mine."

Jenna handed Tashina a jacket. "Where's he now?"

"I don't know. If he gots any brains in his head, he be locked in his room."

Tashina knocked. "Moe, you in there?" She tried the door. It was locked. "Moe, if you in there, jus stay put— and keep your door locked. We gonna find Father John."

They waited to hear Moe moan before they continued on their mission.

They were twenty feet from the rectory when Karter, Eddie, and Sam accosted them.

"Where you off to in such a rush?" Karter stood between Eddie and Sam.

"Let us by, Karter. We gots business wit Father John."

"Your business is our business, Tashina. We're all in this together—or maybe you forgot that little item."

Tashina stood her ground ready to fight. "Let us by, Karter. I ain't gonna tell ya again!"

"I didn't figure you to give up so easy, Tashina. It ain't over yet!" His solid stance, she knew, was meant as a dare to move. "You gonna let us in on what's happening here? We got a right to know."

Tashina figured she didn't have much chance of breaking the stalemate when Karter and the other two boys moved in a line toward the girls. "All right, Karter, all right!" She raised the palms of her hands toward him. "But it's jus gonna be the seven a us. Maria, Melissa, an Moe stays put where they be safe from the likes a you."

"OK, Tashina, I give you that one." Karter motioned to the other boys to back off.

Tashina sent Jenna to collect Demon, who had been waiting for Melissa in a classroom. Everyone else convened in the convent's parlor.

The swearing, shouting, fist-pounding, and foot-stomping went on for half an hour before Bob Sweeney came into the room. "OK, kids, what's going on in here?"

Tashina was shocked when a calm, in-control Karter replied politely and respectfully, "Look, Mr. Sweeney, we got a problem here, and we're just trying to work it out. Could you just please give us a little private time? There ain't gonna be no trouble, you have my word."

"Well, I guess—but I'll be right next door here if you need me." Bob scanned the room. He made eye contact with each of the kids individually. "If any of you need me, just yell and I'll come running. Understand?"

Jenna replied, "Thanks, Mr. Sweeney."

After Bob Sweeney left, Karter was the first to talk. "I ain't giving up that easy. I say, we're all in this together. We all get a say. Any of you got a problem with the concept of abortion?"

The only dissenter in the group was Demon.

"You're outvoted, Demon. Democratic process, majority wins."

Jenna sprang to her feet and shouted. "Hold on, Karter. The only person that's got a vote that counts is Maria, and she's already voted."

"Yeah." Karter's thumbs were hooked into his back pockets. He leaned forward and snarled. "There are ways to get people to change their way of voting, Miss Know-It-All Stein."

"We gots ourselves enough trouble right here. We don't need no more a your violence, Karter Johnson. Ya should know by now, it don't solve nothin!"

"How stupid do you think I am, Tashina?" He put the palms of his hands in the air and strutted over to face her, nose to nose. "Give me a break here. Anything happens to Maria, I'm gonna be the first one they come looking for." He glanced over his shoulder at Demon and turned back to face Tashina. "I want that prize money, maybe more than the rest of you, but I ain't gonna risk doing time to get it."

Tashina turned her back on Karter and motioned to the twins. "C'mon. Let's get this over. We gots to talk to the Father."

The three of them headed for the door.

Eddie ran around in front of them to block their exit. He waved his hands at their faces. "Listen, you guys. Maybe Karter's got something—you got a plan, Karter?"

"Maybe."

Tashina hesitated. Karter's voice had regained the previous uncharacteristic calm. *He be actin mighty smug. Dats not like him. What he gots up his sleeve?* She turned back to face him and shook her head. "Dis better be good."

"A week, that's all I'm asking. If she don't change her mind in a week, we go to the good Father, all of us—all of us together. The Schuster guy, he said, we all win, or we all lose—together."

Tashina and Karter stood facing each other with their hands on their hips.

"None a your rough stuff?"

"You got my word, Tashina."

"Why should we go round trustin you alla sudden?"

"I got as much to lose as you. We all win, or we all lose—together."

The two glowered at each other in silence until Becca interjected, "You going to tell us your plan, Karter?" She sounded determined.

"It's a long shot." Karter cupped his hands behind his head, turned away from Tashina's scowl and fixed his gaze on Eddie. "I'm thinking of taking Maria home to meet my family. It might sober her up a little."

Tashina caught the shrewd look in Eddie's eyes as he raised his brows and nodded at Karter. "I know your family, but what makes you think she'll go?"

Chapter Fourteen

Karter turned back to Tashina. "I could use a little help from my friends here. You could talk her into coming, Tashina."

"I don't get it, Karter. What your family gots to do wit it anyhow?"

"I'll let Eddie fill you in on that one. I'm done talking." With that said, Karter put his hands in his back pockets and marched out of the room.

*****

An hour later, Tashina was back in Maria's room. Melissa was still there, but as usual, she remained quietly in the background—easy to ignore.

Tashina conceded that Karter did indeed want Maria to get a secret abortion. That fact was too obvious to deny.

Maria was still lying on her bed. Tashina sat on the edge, rubbing her back and explaining what Karter wanted her to do.

Maria sat up and blew her nose. "The idea of going to Karter Johnson's house for dinner is about as crazy as you can get, Tashina."

"Nobody can make ya do nothin ya jus ain't gonna do. The one thing dat make sense is he promised to back off if ya do dis. If you do dis, Maria, Karter will go to Father John wit the rest a us."

Maria reached for another tissue. "What happens if I don't? What'll he do then?"

Tashina shrugged. "I ain't got dat one covered."

"I suppose I owe everyone that much." Maria sighed. "What can it hurt to wait another week? There's no rush." She shook her head. "I'm not going to do what he wants, anyway."

Tashina didn't feel too good about betraying her friend. Here she was, encouraging Maria to cave in to Karter's demand when she'd put so much effort into trying to get Maria to stand up for herself.

Tashina took a deep breath. *I gots a stake in dis, too. What if Karter's plan does work? Wouldn't we all be better off for it? Dis time, I think I be on Karter's side—damn!*

Maria interrupted Tashina's thoughts. "At least now he won't hit on me. I sure don't trust him, though."

"Whatever he gots in his head, he ain't gonna hurt ya, Maria. He might be bad, but he ain't gonna put his own butt in jeopardy." *Again...*

In the end, Maria agreed to go on the condition that Moe go with her, and Karter accepted the terms.

*****

That Friday, when the kids were dropped off on the school grounds, the unlikely combination of Karter, Maria, and Moe walked together to Karter's house. Once inside, Karter introduced his mother to his friends. "Take their coats, Karter. Didn't I teach you manners?"

He hung the coats in the hall closet. "Hey, Ma, what's a good-looking girl like you doing in a place like this?"

Carol smiled at Karter's boyish teasing. "That priest must have worked some kind of miracle on you, Karter.

You haven't brought friends home for dinner since you were eight years old."

"Aw, Ma, I just didn't want to share my beautiful mother with a bunch of losers." He pulled her apron string and laughed.

Carol slapped Karter's hand away playfully. "Your father won't be here tonight. His truck broke down in Peoria. He has to stay with it." Carol was smiling so hard, Karter thought she'd break her cheeks. "I sure wish he could see you with your friends, honey. He'd be so pleased."

Karter was gratified by the puzzled looks he saw Maria and Moe exchange when Kathryn came out of the bedroom, made a beeline for Carol, put her arms around her mother, and begged for the affection she could always count on.

He quietly watched the familiar scene. *Go for it, sis. Put on a good show for my friends here.*

"Why can't I marry Rodney, Mama? He likes me. I know he likes me. He kisses me all the time." She twisted her mother's hair and patted her arm.

Carol stroked her daughter's head.

"Kathryn, honey. I told you that just yesterday. You're different. You're just a dear sweet child, and you're your mama's little girl."

Mother and daughter stood hugging one another, seemingly oblivious to their audience. "It's always gonna be that way, honey."

Carol released her grip and gently pushed Kathryn away. She shook her head and pointed her finger as she scolded the girl as if she were five years old instead of fifteen.

"Now, didn't I tell you to stay away from that Rodney boy?"

"I know," Kathryn moaned in a little baby voice.

"You heard me, honey." She gave Kathryn a gentle shove. "Now, go set the table. Karter and his friends here are hungry, and we have to show them what good hosts we are."

As if noticing for the first time that there was someone else in the room, Kathryn glommed onto Karter.

He held her at arm's length. "Kathryn." Karter's voice was gentle. "Mama told you to set the table now, didn't she?"

Kathryn gave her mother a pleading look. "I did my work already today, Mama. I'm tired."

Carol had finished half the job herself by now. "Say hello to Karter's friends, Kathryn."

Kathryn tried to hug Moe, but Moe grabbed her hands instead. "Hello, Kathryn, it is very nice to meet you."

Maria had a baffled look on her face. She took a step back as Kathryn approached her. "Hello, Kathryn." She extended her hand, and Kathryn shook it politely before turning back to her table-setting chore.

"He kisses me, Mama, he does, and he wants to marry me and have babies with me." She cocked her head at Karter. "He said so, Karter. He did, you know."

"Sure, Kathryn, he said so…" He looked at the ceiling and then glanced at his guests.

"Where's Kirsten tonight, Ma?" Karter asked while Kathryn hummed to herself and continued to put silverware haphazardly on the table.

Chapter Fourteen

"He's staying at a friend's house." Carol took a pot from the stove and scraped the potatoes into a serving bowl with a rubber spatula. "With a boy you don't know, honey. Come sit down. Dinner's ready." She motioned to Moe and Maria to take their seats at the table.

Carol passed the platter to Moe, and they all started serving themselves. "Now, tell me about your friends, Karter. Maria. What a pretty name." She smiled, and Maria politely smiled back. "I'm so happy my Karter has such lovely friends. And Moe, is that your real name, Moe?"

"It is shortened from Mohandas, Mrs. Johnson. It is an Indian name."

"I see—but Mohandas is such a nice-sounding name. Maybe you should consider being called Mohandas. Would you mind if I call you Mohandas?" She handed the potatoes to him.

"No, ma'am." Moe took the dish from Carol and scooped some mashed potatoes onto his plate.

"All right then, Mohandas. I hope you like beefsteak. I know a lot of Indian people are vegetarian." She looked at her son. "Karter, you should have told me."

"It is very fine for me, Mrs. Johnson. I like beefsteak."

Karter reached for the potatoes. "Moe here doesn't go in for Indian food, Mama. He likes American-style. American-style food—and American-style girls." He shot a mean-spirited look at Moe. "Ain't that right, Moe?"

Maria and Moe silently picked at their food. Karter held back a snicker when he saw his mother looking at them with a puzzled expression on her face. He almost laughed out loud when Moe grabbed his knife, cut away at the hunk of meat on his plate, and shoved a large piece in his mouth. "This is very fine beefsteak, Mrs. Johnson. Thank you for inviting us."

Kathryn seemed unconcerned, deeply concentrating on getting as much food as she could, as fast as she could. She filled her mouth too full, and some dropped back to her plate. She breathed through her mouth and made loud smacking noises.

Karter was accustomed to his sister's eating habits. He was counting on her to educate his innocent guests to the facts of life. *Yeah, take a real good look, my naïve little friends. I hope you learn a very important lesson here tonight—one that could benefit all of us.*

After dinner, Kathryn went back to her bedroom. They heard her singing off-key along with Puff the Magic Dragon, and Carol began clearing the table.

"I can help with that, Mrs. Johnson." Maria collected some dishes and carried them to the sink. She turned the faucet on and began rinsing.

"No, no." She gently shoved Maria aside. "You kids entertain yourselves. I can handle the dishes myself. Karter, we could put the board on the table if you and your friends want to play ping pong."

"C'mon, Ma," Karter teased. "I brought my friends here to show off what a pretty lady my mom is. The dishes can wait." He tugged at her sleeve. "Sit and talk with us, Ma."

"You kids don't want to be bothered with an old lady."

"You're not so old, Ma." Karter purposely put a sardonic twinkle in his eyes.

"You just go on, now." She gave Karter a gentle shove toward the living room.

Karter turned around and scowled at her. His voice was resolute, his manner inflexible. "I said the dishes can wait, Ma."

"Maybe we should go now." Moe scurried to the hall, grabbed his jacket from the closet, and fumbled around to find Maria's.

"I ain't done with you yet." Karter grabbed the coats from Moe's grip. "You owe me." He threw the jackets on the floor and directed his guests toward the couch in the living room.

Maria and Moe obediently took their places next to each other.

Carol reluctantly settled herself into one of the easy chairs, like a child who'd been told that no wasn't an option. "What would you like me to talk about, Karter?" She stared vacantly into space.

"I want you to tell my friends here how old you are." Karter's voice was rough, and he glared at his mother.

"I'm thirty-one, Karter. You could have told them that yourself."

Karter continued to glare at his mother. "You're not one of those vain women who lies about her age, are you, Ma?"

"No, Karter." She looked up toward the ceiling as though there were answers there. "I don't lie about anything, Karter. You know that." She returned Karter's scowl. "It's against the Lord's will to lie."

"How old is Kathryn?"

"She's fifteen, Karter. What are you getting at?"

Karter was keenly aware of his audience as he continued to play out the drama for their benefit. He and his mother remained locked in a standoff. *You know very well what I'm getting at, mother.* "That means you were fifteen when you got pregnant with her, right? Tell my friends here what's wrong with Kathryn, Ma, and how she got to be the way she is."

"I don't know why you want me to do this, Karter, but it's no secret." Carol sighed. She looked first at Maria, and then at Moe, before she spoke. "Kathryn has a condition called Down's Syndrome. It's my understanding that the mother's eggs—eggs that are either too old or too young—cause the condition." Her voice sounded like she was reading from a textbook. She turned back to Karter. "Is that what you wanted me to say, Karter?"

"Yeah. Thanks, Ma." He turned to Maria. "I guess we'll be going now. I'll just walk my friends home." Karter retrieved the coats from the floor and started to help Maria on with hers. Moe grabbed the coat out of his hands and held it for Maria.

Once outside, Moe said to Karter, "There is no need to walk with us, Karter. We got the picture."

Karter stood on the porch watching as Maria and Moe walked down the street, hand in hand. He was pleased with himself. *You may not know it, but I just did you guys a big favor.* He smirked at them before going back in to get his own jacket.

*****

Chapter Fourteen

Maria and Moe walked in silence for a few blocks before Moe spoke. "There is a test that you can take, Maria. If it were to be Down's Syndrome, then what would you do? Would you agree—would you do what it is that they would like you to do?"

A cold shiver passed through Maria's body as she voiced the question to which she feared she already knew the answer. "You want me to do it too, just like the rest of them, don't you, Moe?"

"It is not only about the money, Maria. We are very young. How would we be able to manage it?"

She yanked her hand from his. Close to tears, she turned to face him. "It's still a life, Moe. It's just as wrong to kill a baby like that as it is to kill a normal one."

Moe's mouth gaped open, but no words escaped.

Maria felt very sure of herself as she stood up for her principles. "I only got two things out of Karter's little trick: one more thing to worry about, and where you stand." As she walked away from him, she moaned. "I'm tired. I'm just gonna go home and talk to my mother."

Moe shouted after her, "You made a promise, Maria."

"I kept my word. I went to Karter's little dinner party." She called over her shoulder.

Moe ran to catch up and grabbed her hand to stop her. "You promised Karter—and the rest of us, too. You said that you would wait until Monday—when we can all have a time to decide how to handle it. Karter came through with no violence. If you tell now, he will think that you have broken your promise. I do not know what it is he will do then. You will not be safe, Maria. Maria, listen to me…"

Maria sighed. She thought her heart would break. *Tashina was right. He's not worried about me, or about our baby. He's worried about his own skin. He's just like the rest.* "I guess I can wait two more days. But my mind's made up."

Moe looked down and shuffled from one foot to the other. "I have also made a promise—to my brother. I intend to keep my promise, at least until Monday."

"I don't think you're going to get the kind of miracle you're hoping for, Moe, but I guess a promise is a promise."

When they got to Maria's door, Moe made a move to kiss her goodnight. She gently pushed him away. "I'm sorry, Moe. I couldn't love a guy who would kill a baby."

Maria held back the tears as she watched Moe walk away with his shoulders drooping.

Chapter Fifteen
Bad News Can Wait
March 1997

"What's this? Why aren't you in class?" A bewildered John, still in his robe and slippers, faced the ten teenagers at his door.

Jenna spoke for the group. "We can't take Mr. Schuster's money, Father. We broke the rules—all of them."

I knew it. John felt the tightness in his chest as he scanned the blank faces before him. "And now, you've come for my help?"

Demon answered simply, "Yes, Father."

"All of you, go back to the convent." He shooed them off. "I'll meet with you in the dining room as soon as I'm dressed." He watched them as they turned and slowly shuffled away in silence.

When he arrived at the convent, he found the students quietly waiting. They had left the chair at the head of the table vacant.

John felt at home in his role as counselor. His manner was compassionate, and he heard them all, each in turn, correcting one another, adding pieces that were missed, sometimes disagreeing with how it all happened. When they'd finished, he whispered, perhaps just loud enough to be heard by some, "Guess I'm the safety net after all."

The first decision John made was to send Maria home to her parents. He knew she had more telling to do, and she needed medical attention—the sooner the better. He wasn't surprised at the puzzled look on Maria's face when he said, "I'll expect you back in school next Monday, though. Pregnancy is not considered a major illness; therefore, you will be expected to finish out the semester. At least that's one rule that hasn't been broken. Stay here with the others, Maria, until I can arrange for Mrs. Sweeney to take you home.

"Moe, you'd better go home too. You have some explaining to do as well. Mrs. Sweeney can take you both."

Moe contemplated his feet. "Yes, Father."

"You won't be needing a whole week, Moe. You can call Mrs. Sweeney to pick you up when you're ready to come back."

John took his cell phone from his pocket. "What is your number, Maria?" He dialed the numbers as she said them. "Hello, Mrs. Guliano, this is Father John Murphy. I'm calling to let you know that I'm sending Maria home…She has something very important to discuss with you…Yes, well, she can tell you that in person. She will be needing your advice and counsel…"

He made a similar call to Moe's father and called Mrs. Sweeney in from the kitchen.

"Can you drive Maria and Moe to their homes?"

"Sure, Father. I have some shopping to do in Milwaukee, anyhow."

"Can you bring the car around to the front door in about ten minutes?"

"I'll just finish up in the kitchen and get my coat, Father."

With that done, he turned his attention back to the somber group and spoke with conviction.

"The semester will continue with business as usual. I will have a conference with Mr. Schuster. After all, the final decision is still his."

John looked around at the stunned faces of his charges. "Yes, you heard me right. We will continue here as usual, until we are told to do otherwise by Mr. Schuster. Are there any questions?"

John was faced with a small sea of blank expressions.

"The whole purpose of this experiment was to discover the secret of what happens between bullies and victims. Even if you must forfeit the prize for breaking the rules, you still have an obligation to Mr. Schuster. He has, after all, financed your education for a year. He's kept his part of the bargain. Now, you must keep yours."

Karter and Eddie exchanged a look of bewilderment. Maria had tears in her eyes. When he saw Tashina's contorted face, John thought, *She looks like her brain hurts.*

The twins were locked into their private language of knowing gestures.

"You will use the rest of your time here to prepare to tell Mr. Schuster what you've learned from your adventures in our experimental school. I don't mean what you've learned in math or science. I mean what you've learned about bullies and victims. You owe him that much." John noticed the puzzled look on Melissa's face. "We will, of course, have classes as usual."

Mrs. Sweeney pulled up in the lot to collect Maria and Moe. "The rest of you can go to your classes now."

After they'd left the convent and headed toward the school, John went back his office in the rectory. He sat at his desk with his head in his hands. *Confession is a good thing. They will all sleep better tonight. And now it's my turn to tell.*

Once again, John picked up the phone and dialed.

Kevin answered, "Mr. Schuster's residence."

"Hello, Kevin, this is John Murphy. I need to talk to Mr. Schuster. It's pretty important."

"Just a moment, sir."

Sydney's voice came on, "Hello, John. What's up? The news must be bad, or you wouldn't be calling."

John sighed. "We need to talk, Syd. Your place or mine?"

"I'll be in Milwaukee next week Thursday. Can it wait until then?"

"I guess that would be OK."

"We can meet in Denise's office. It's quiet there in the evening. What's this all about, John? Has something happened at the school?"

"I think it would be better if we talk in person. Thursday of next week then?"

"I could change some plans—meet sooner if it's urgent."

"No, it's not urgent…" *That will give some time for the dust to settle.* "Thursday will be fine."

"All right then, let's say four."

"Right, I'll see you then."

*****

John's call weighed heavily on Sydney's mind. *I shouldn't have gotten my hopes up like that. A bunch of loser kids from the inner city…what did I think they could teach me anyhow? I should have heeded Denise's warning. It's never going to be any different. The bullies will always push weaker, more sensitive people around.* He sighed. *Bad news doesn't just go away, but at least it can wait. I need a distraction.*

He dialed Denise's number and invited her to a weekend in New York. "We could fly out Friday night, take in a couple of plays, and come back Sunday."

"Oh, Syd, I'd love to, but I can't leave Melissa here all by herself for the whole weekend."

Sydney was not in a mood to be put off. "What do you say to me coming there, then?"

When Denise didn't respond, Sydney went on. "We could play like an old married couple and veg out in front of the television."

"That would be real nice, Syd. We'd play house."

Denise's voice didn't sound very welcoming, but Sydney didn't want to accept no for an answer. "I can think of a lot worse things to do…"

Denise didn't answer.

"Denise? Denise, are you there?"

"Well, why not?"

She still sounded tentative. Sydney sighed. "Denise, if you don't want me there…"

Syd was relieved when Denise responded more enthusiastically. "We're consenting adults, aren't we? If Melissa is going to fit into my life, she's going to have to accept that I have one. I'd be delighted to have you for a weekend guest, Sydney. I'm a pretty good cook, you know—maybe not as good as Kevin, but—"

"I'll be looking forward to it, Denise. The time will drag until Friday."

Sydney sat back in his chair and wondered what it would be like to spend a weekend with Denise—and Melissa. One thing was for certain: he was determined it would be pleasant. *If our weekend in Door County was any indication, she's attracted to me, too. I could have made love to her then if I hadn't been such a cautious sourpuss.*

*****

On Friday afternoon, Melissa hesitated outside Denise's office door. She heard the strangest thing. Denise was singing "Some Enchanted Evening." She sounded like a schoolgirl as she belted out, "Fly to his side, and make him your own."

Melissa tapped on the door, and the singing stopped. "That you, Melissa? Come in. I'm just about ready to leave."

Melissa was expecting some sort of explanation, but Denise just smiled and gathered some things from the desk.

In the car, Melissa was surprised and a little nervous as Denise matter-of-factly filled her in on the weekend plans.

"Sydney? That's the Mr. Schuster that was going to give us the prize money, isn't it?"

"Yes, that's him. Did you say 'was'? *Was* going to give you the prize money?" Denise slammed on the brakes and pulled over to the curb. She parked the car and turned toward Melissa.

"We won't be getting it," Melissa blurted out the words quickly. "We broke the rules."

"I haven't heard anything about that. What happened?"

Melissa took a deep breath and went on. "Before the big meeting with Father John, the only rule I knew about being broken was the one about a girl getting pregnant. Maria Guliano. Moe Shastri's the father."

"No…I don't believe it. Maria, the little Italian girl who always runs away from trouble, and Moe Shastri, the Indian boy—the nice little Indian boy, the one who loves the cafeteria food?"

Melissa fidgeted with the strap on her backpack as she explained. "They said it was consensual. I mean, they both agreed. But that doesn't matter. Mr. Schuster said that if any girl in the program got pregnant before the end of the experiment, no one would get the prize. So that's it, then—I never really thought we'd get it anyway."

"I wouldn't be too sure." Denise turned her head toward the window on her side of the car. She sounded more like she was thinking out loud than talking to Melissa. "He might bend a little—that is, if he gets what he's looking for…"

"But that isn't the only rule that got broken."

"Oh?" Denise turned back and faced Melissa.

"They broke them all—well, all except one. They might have been able to keep the others a secret, but not the pregnancy. They tried to talk Maria into an abortion, but it's against her religion and she wouldn't hear of it."

"Interesting. I wonder if Sydney—ah, Mr. Schuster—knows about this."

"Father John said he was going to call him right after our meeting."

"Then he already knows. Hmm…. I hope this doesn't put a damper on the weekend."

Denise was about to start the engine when Melissa tugged on her sleeve. "There's more."

Denise frowned and shook her head. "That must have been some meeting. Go on, Melissa, tell me the rest."

"Father John gave us an assignment. He said no one was to leave the program. That's one rule that hasn't been broken yet. He said we were to try to figure out what we've learned from our experience—I mean about bullies and victims—so we could tell Mr. Schuster when the time comes. He said we owed him that much. I guess Father John's right. I'm not sure what I've learned, though."

"One thing I can say for you, Melissa. When you showed up on my doorstep, you did the right thing. When you're a victim and you're in more danger than you can handle, the best thing is to get help from a trusted adult." Denise shuddered. "Your whole life could have been ruined through no fault of your own."

"There aren't that many of them around, Ms. H— trustworthy adults, I mean. Some are OK, but not many are willing to give you the kind of help you really need." Melissa felt the lump in her throat, and she tried to hold back the tears, but the tears wouldn't take no for an answer. "I guess I just got lucky. I picked the right one," she sobbed.

While the older woman and the almost-woman were locked in a comforting embrace, Melissa thought about her mother's tears—hopeless tears—helpless tears. Melissa knew her mother loved her, but with Denise, it was different. Her tears carried a message of hope. Melissa didn't just feel loved in Denise's arms—she felt safe.

After about ten minutes of wordless sobbing, they dried their eyes and composed themselves. Denise started the engine, and they continued the rest of their ride home in silence.

As they pulled into the driveway, Denise glanced at Melissa over her shoulder. "I could use some help with dinner tonight. I want it to be special. How about it?"

"Sure, but I've never cooked before. You'll have to show me." Melissa flashed Denise a timid smile.

*****

Sydney took the liberty of letting himself in, and in a pleasant, teasing voice he yelled from the front door, "Hi, honey, I'm home."

He went straight for the kitchen, where Denise was stirring the risotto and Melissa was cleaning the shrimp. The music in the background was Chopin. "How sweet it is." Sydney did a Jackie Gleason routine, and Denise laughed.

With the flowers still in his hand, he embraced Denise and kissed her on the lips.

Out of the corner of his eye, he caught Melissa blushing and turning her face away from them. He gave Denise a cheek peck and tapped Melissa on the shoulder. "Hello, Melissa. How are you today?" He handed her the flowers. "Could you please find a vase for these while I give my wife another kiss?" He sang, "Haven't felt like this, my dear, since can't remember when—it's been a long, long time."

Denise wrapped her arms around him, and they tripped the light fantastic around the kitchen table.

Sydney inhaled the intoxicating aromas emanating from the kettles on the stove. "Smells good. What's for dinner? What's on television?" He kissed her again.

"Oh, Ozzie, you're just too much, but in front of the children..." Denise turned to give Melissa a wink.

An obviously dumbfounded Melissa stood with the bouquet in one hand and a vase in the other. "Uh, will this be OK, Mr. Schuster?"

Sydney took the flowers from Melissa, waved them in the air, brought his arm down across his waist, and bowed. "This will be just fine, my lovely lady."

Even Melissa laughed out loud at that one.

Sydney put the flowers on the counter, took the vase to the sink, and turned the spigot on. "Melissa, we're going to have to do something about that Mr. Schuster thing. I want you to call me Sydney, or Syd, but only when we're at home." He shook his finger in the air and tried to sound like an authoritarian father. "At more formal occasions, I will expect Mr. Schuster, just like from all the other students."

Melissa looked a little doubtful as she nodded her consent.

"How about you, Denise? What does she call you?"

Melissa answered. Her voice sounded meek. "I call her Ms. H."

"Ms. H has a nice ring, but it sounds a little stiff." Sydney stuffed a shrimp in his mouth. "Mom is too presumptuous, perhaps for both of you. I'm not sure I could handle that, either. How about Denise?" Still chewing, he looked at Denise. "Could you handle that—in private, that is?"

Denise raised her eyebrows. "Denise would be fine. OK with you, Melissa?"

Melissa signaled her approval with a smile.

Dinner came with the small talk that you might overhear at any dinner table in the USA—in the 1970s, that is. They were playing, all three of them. Melissa even laughed at Sydney's corny jokes.

Sydney leaned back in his chair, a satisfied smile on his face. "I like playing house."

After dinner, Melissa excused herself and went to her room to read. While Sydney helped with the dishes, Denise asked him if he'd heard from John lately. Sydney kissed her to keep her from talking. "Bad news can wait, Denise. I don't want anything to spoil this weekend. How about some good old-fashioned necking while we watch a movie?"

"You're on."

*****

In her room, Melissa wondered what was going on. Half the time she didn't know what they were talking about, especially these Ozzie and Harriet people they kept referring to, but she liked it. She felt safe with them—both of them.

Melissa had had nothing but negative experiences with men in her young life, but she'd read enough books to know it wasn't always like that. That wasn't what confused her. She plumped her pillow and switched the light off. *It's just…they're so old.*

*****

Chapter Fifteen

The next night, Sydney and Denise switched off the television early.

Sydney felt comfortable—an "at home" feeling—when Denise snuggled up next to him on the couch. "Do you ever miss having children in your life, Syd?" Her voice sounded warm and inviting.

"I suppose it would be nice if I could have a relationship with my grandchildren."

Sydney felt a twinge of regret as he remembered two bright-eyed little boys—his own progeny. "They're about Melissa's age. I haven't seen them since they were just little tykes."

"Does Simon forbid you to see them?"

"Not in so many words."

Sydney removed his arm from around Denise's shoulder and slouched down with his elbows on his knees. "We tried to stay in touch, but my visits were a disaster."

Denise moved to the chair facing him. "How so?"

"At first Simon and I were guarded but polite. It was implicitly understood that we wouldn't discuss Ruben, money—especially inheritance money—or Simon's 'waste management' business. We talked only about inconsequential things. I suppose we could have talked about football—Simon's an avid fan—but you know where I stand on that subject. Mostly we just let the awkward silence hang between us, like some kind of protective fog."

Denise reached over and touched his hand. "That must have been pretty stressful for both of you."

"A funny thing happens when you try to avoid talking about something." Sydney sighed. "You put so much effort into it that the very thing you want to avoid takes up more and more space in your brain until there's no room for anything else. The next thing you know, without your permission, the words spill out, words that double-dare you to stifle them. Hurtful, mean, nasty, angry words that won't allow themselves to be taken back—you want to say, 'I really didn't mean that,' but you know you did. You just didn't mean to *say* it. Not talking at all is better."

Sydney sank back into the couch. *She sure has a way of getting me to talk.*

Denise returned to her position next to him on the couch and cuddled close again. They sat quietly for a moment before Denise asked, "What about your grandsons? They should have provided a distraction."

"I couldn't take it, Denise. I thought Simon played with them too roughly. The littlest one, Jacob, looked terrified when Simon flung him into the air—they were just babies, but Simon was already ordering them around as though they were his appendages."

Denise sighed. "Your grandsons are missing out on a good grandfather."

"I wonder what they look like now. I haven't gotten so much as a picture. They'd be eleven and thirteen." Sydney sat up straight and stretched. "Anyway, it works both ways. Simon could call me; he could be the one to make the first move. He could at least send pictures, for God's sake."

Denise reached over and rubbed his back.

"Mmm, that feels good."

"It's late; let's go to bed."

Chapter Fifteen

Sydney stayed with Denise and Melissa in Milwaukee until Monday morning. During the day, Denise, Sydney, and Melissa were a threesome. Like tourists, they visited the art museum and the domes, places Melissa had never been. At night, Melissa made herself scarce. They didn't mention the project again—not since Friday, when Syd said bad news could wait.

Chapter Sixteen
Settling the Score
April 1997

Maria got lucky. All signs indicated it was a healthy fetus, and she had the support of her family to keep the baby or to put it up for adoption.

She was concerned about how things had gone for Moe when he told his family about the baby. But they were not holding hands at sunset on that mild April evening as they strolled along the road to the Falls. The comfort they'd felt with each other in a more innocent time had been swapped for tension—tension created by a problem with which neither was prepared to cope.

After hearing Maria's good news, Moe responded, "I am happy for you, Maria—for you and for the baby."

"How did it go for you at home, with your family, Moe, when you told them?"

"It might have been many times more difficult. I am grateful that Jahan was there to help to sort things out. The meeting with both of our families present was the worst. I could not look in the face of your mother, Maria."

"Yeah, telling her was hard for me too—because I let her down..." Maria knew her mother wanted more for her than the kind of life her mother had accepted for herself—by default.

After a moment of awkward silence, she went on. "Still, I always knew I could count on her support. It was my dad that worried me. I was afraid he'd kill you."

"I could not fault him for his feelings, Maria. I am the one to be blamed. I have been weak. I have agreed with our parents. We are too young to become married."

"Don't be so hard on yourself, Moe."

They walked in silence for a few moments before Maria risked asking the big question, the one that robbed her of sleep. "Do you still think about," she hesitated, "suicide?"

"No." Moe was quick to answer. "I have hurt too many people already—because of my weakness."

"It wasn't just us. The rest of them broke some rules too, you know."

Moe picked up a stone and tossed it into the road.

"I would really appreciate the prize money—now more than ever, if I am expected to support a child and, at the same time, expected to figure out the puzzles of my own future."

Maria flinched. True to form, she held back on expressing her own hurt feelings and listened to his instead.

When they reached the Dairy Queen, Moe slowed. "There is something else on my mind, Maria. Could we stop here for a cola while I explain it to you?"

Chapter Sixteen

After ordering black cows, they settled themselves across from each other in a booth.

Maria waited anxiously for Moe to explain the somber look on his face. *What could be worse than what we've already been through?* she wondered.

"Eddie gave me a lecture on safe sex, and he wasn't talking just about babies, Maria. He said to me, 'So far, all you've got to worry about is a baby, and that's mostly Maria's problem.'"

Moe's words, "that's mostly Maria's problem," echoed in her ears, and when he reached for her hand across the table, Maria pulled back.

"Eddie said to me," Moe went on ""It could have been AIDS, you know.' I asked him, 'What is it that you are talking about, Eddie?'" Moe whispered, "He was very agitated—he scared me, Maria."

She leaned forward to hear him better. "I'm not sure I know what you're getting at Moe. What else did Eddie say?"

"He kept saying AIDS so many times. He said it is a disease that is transmitted through sexual acts, it breaks down the immune system and makes you vulnerable to all viruses and germs. Eddie said, 'Once you got AIDS, it's only a matter of time, man.'"

Moe risked another reach for Maria's hand. Once again she pulled back, but she listened with heightened interest as he continued to tell her what Eddie said.

"I told him it was the first time for both of us, and that I had learned my lesson well. He said I ought to get myself checked out. I don't think he believed me, about it being our first time—I wanted to hit him for what he was thinking about you, Maria."

Moe's eyes were glistening with bottled-up tears. Maria's own tears were begging for liberation. Still, she held back.

"He also told me that you can get the virus by using drugs that are ingested through a needle. I looked it up in a medical dictionary, Maria. He is correct in what he told me." Moe took a deep breath. "It was good of him to tell me. If you have doubts, Maria, you should get yourself checked out."

"What are you telling me, Moe? Do you have AIDS?" She spoke so loudly that the heads of other customers turned.

Moe put a finger to his lips. "Shh." He looked around and answered in a whisper. "No, Maria, I do not have it. It was the first time for me, too. And I have never ingested any drugs through a needle. I have been so weak and stupid that there is no reason for you to trust what I am saying. If it will give you peace of mind, Maria, you should get yourself checked by the doctor."

Moe reached for Maria's hand again. This time, she relented. "I don't need to get checked out. I believe you, Moe."

That night, after bed check, Maria turned out her nightlight and lay in her bed with her eyes open. *You're wrong, Tashina. He does care about me. He's not like the rest.* Still, she couldn't forget he wanted her to abort their child. They would not be getting married—now or ever.

And, there would be no more cooking lessons in the kitchen.

*****

"Hey, white boy!" Tashina barked at Karter when she found him coming out of his room on his way to the bathroom. "We still got some settlin up to do."

She was pleased to catch him looking around to see if anyone else was in earshot before he answered, "OK, OK, Tashina. I'm sorry."

"Yeah—dat ain't good nuff. Jus what is it you sorry bout, Karter Johnson?" She stood with one hip jutted out to the side as she waited for his response.

"You're not gonna make it easy on me, are you, Tashina?" Karter kicked at the carpet. "You want me to get on my knees?" He looked down at his feet and mumbled. "I guess I'm sorry for hitting on you."

"No, dat ain't it! I can handle dat. It what you did later, wit Rick Guliano, is what I'm talkin bout here." She leaned toward him with her hands on her hips.

"Yeah, well, I really am sorry about that—" He jerked his head back and rolled his eyes. "But you ain't so all-fired innocent here either, Tashina. You didn't have no cause to come at me with that knife. I'll admit I was out of line, I was a little drunk, but I wouldn't have hurt you—you should have known that. But you came at me with a knife! That's what made me so ticked off. But I guess I had it coming—"

"Ya damned right ya did. OK, I gave you back twice. I'm gonna give ya dat one. Right now, I'm waitin for ya to pologize for the big one. Dat thing you did wit Rick—dat ain't just givin back twice. Dat be more like three, maybe four times. Dat was revenge. Dat was evil!" Tashina stood her ground as she scowled at him.

"I'm sorry…" Karter took a deep breath. "What made you stop him? By all rights you should have been helping Rick, not me." His voice was soft and contrite.

"I don't know, Karter. Guess it jus gotta stop somewheres. I been thinkin, maybe once is enough—maybe dat's where it gotta stop."

"Yeah." Karter shuffled his feet. "We settled up now?"

"I guess—ya still owes one to Maria though, and I'm holdin ya to it." Tashina turned her back and walked away.

Later that evening, Tashina flipped the television off to get the attention of the other girls. "It ain't often we all's in the same room wit no boys present."

She was in good form as she filled them in on her adventures with Karter. Her voice was loud and commanding. "I tol dat Karter Johnson a thing or two. I tol him once is enough!"

Becca Stein's eyes lit up. "That's just like in the Torah—'an eye for an eye.'"

Maria started to protest, but Becca cut her off. "Lots of people don't understand that. They say, 'Yeah sure, we'll have a whole bunch of blind, toothless people around.' But it's not like that—"

Jenna jumped in. "We might have a few one-eyed people and some teeth missing, but they wouldn't be dead! See it's *one* eye for one eye and *one* tooth for one tooth—"

Becca had her mouth open to talk when Jenna stopped her with one of those looks and went on to say, "A guy knocks out one of your teeth; you don't take a whole mouth full in return. You take one!"

Tashina was exhilarated by the validation of her point of view. "Jus like I said." She jumped up and down like a banshee. "Once is enough! Maybe I be a Jew and don't even know it." She slapped her thigh. "Ain't dat a good one, lil ol black girl Tashina Jones a Jew?"

Tashina and the twins were laughing so hard, tears came to their eyes. Their laughter was abruptly aborted, however, when they heard Maria shout. "No! You got it all wrong! Jesus said to turn the other cheek!"

The others stood with their mouths hanging open, but Tashina wasn't surprised by her friend's frenzied outburst. She turned to Maria and spoke seriously with authority in her voice. "Where's dat got you, Maria?"

Maria cringed. She looked at Tashina through damp eyes. "I don't know. Jesus said to turn the other cheek; that's what it says in the Bible…"

Tashina shook her head back and forth slowly. *She still don't get it.* She spoke softly, compassionately this time. "How many cheeks you got, girl?" Out of the corner of her eye, she saw Melissa nodding. *At least dat one's gettin it.*

*****

The next day, Karter saw Maria sitting at the table in the dining room with a book open and a pen in her hand. She was alone. A few weeks ago, he would have taken the opportunity to play his little games with her. Instead, he straddled a chair beside her.

"I gotta hand it to you, Maria. You stood your ground. I still think you're stupid to mess up your life with a kid and all, but you stood up for what you believe."

Maria looked up from her book. She had a stunned expression on her face as Karter continued. "Tashina said I owe you an apology, and I guess I do, but you gotta learn a little something about life here—I mean real life. You lie down like a rug, and you're just asking to be walked on."

Maria sounded nervous, almost apologetic, as she whined, "That doesn't give you the right to just take advantage, Karter—nobody deserves to be walked on."

Karter spoke gently, "Maybe you're right about not deserving and all that—but that's how it works. You just keep giving, and you can be sure somebody's gonna be there for the taking. Wise up, Maria."

As far as Karter was concerned, he had more than fulfilled his obligation to Tashina. He left Maria to her book and her thoughts.

*****

"When am I supposed to turn the other cheek and when am I supposed to take a tooth?" Maria was sitting on Tashina's bed.

"You gettin better, girl. But you still gots a ways to go."

Maria took some chips from the bag Tashina offered. "I like it better when people are nice to each other." She talked with a mouthful of chips. "I don't get it—if you're supposed to give back what you get, doesn't that mean the nice things, too?"

Tashina carefully thought about what Maria said before she responded. "I gotta admit, you gots a point there, girl."

"And don't people deserve a second chance?" Maria came back quicker and stronger than usual.

"Oh..." Tashina's own voice, "once is enough," played back in her ears. "I gots to puzzle out how dat one fits in."

Two red eyes stared back at Tashina in the bathroom mirror the next morning. "One tooth for one tooth, one smile for one smile. Dat makes sense. Dat's keepin things even. There gots to be somethin between a bad thing dats been done and gettin a second chance," she told her image in the mirror.

*****

Two days later, they were all present for the group meeting. Melissa wasn't about to become an active participant until she was sure where the others stood. She stayed in the background as she watched and listened.

Karter and Tashina took their customary pot shots at each other over leadership. Eddie backed Karter as usual, and Becca backed Tashina.

The meeting had been in session for about thirty minutes when Jenna explained about the Torah.

Melissa was surprised when Demon jumped out of his chair and said, "I don't get it—all this talk about eyes and teeth." He put the palms of his hands in the air and shrugged. "Somebody fill me in here."

"What is it you don't get?" Karter barked at Demon.

"We still haven't solved the real problem here, Karter." Demon took a deep breath and looked around the table. "I guess we're all getting along with each other better and all that, but let me ask you, Becca." He walked over to her chair and pointed his finger at her nose. "Do you like Karter? Do you like him any more than you did the first day you laid eyes on him?"

"That's not fair, Demon." Becca stood up to meet his eyes. "I don't have to *like* Karter. I'm not going to *marry* him. We'll probably never be friends." Her voice trailed off.

Melissa watched Karter nod in agreement.

Becca quickly glanced over her shoulder at Maria and continued. "Maria and I don't see eye to eye on a lot of things either." She turned back, looked Demon in the eye, and shook her finger in his face. "But here's where I have to agree with Karter: We don't have to like each other or even *agree* with each other about everything."

Karter had a pompous grin on his face.

Melissa was fascinated with how Karter could turn things to his own advantage. She watched the befuddled Demon stammer, "You think we could just get along with each other—even if we don't like each other?"

"Yeah, I do."

The group was silent.

Demon looked confused as he shook his head and settled back into his place at the table.

Melissa knew that Demon didn't like fighting and that he valued friendship over money, but she didn't know he felt so strongly about it.

Maria's timid voice was next to be heard. She addressed her comments to Demon, but she was looking at Tashina. "We don't just have eyes and teeth, Demon. We also have cheeks. Sometimes, it's best to turn them." She sat down quickly.

Encouraged by Maria's assertiveness, Melissa got up on her shaking legs to address her classmates.

All heads turned at the sight of "the quiet one" on her feet—facing them.

"There's one more story to tell." She took a deep breath and continued in a quiet, yet commanding voice.

"Sometimes we can't just work things out by ourselves." She looked to Demon for a nod of agreement before she continued.

When Melissa finished her story, there were some mouths hanging open and some raised eyebrows.

Eddie broke the silence. "You're actually living with Ms. Hanover?" He hit his forehead with the palm of his hand. "Like you're sleeping in her house and eating her food, and having dinner conversations with her? You just went to her house and stayed on her doorstop like a stray cat until she took you in and fed you warm milk?" His eyes swept the faces of the other kids. "I thought she was too old to still have some milk in her." He smirked. "Now I think I heard it all."

Melissa looked down her nose at him. "She's not as old as you might think."

She left out the part about Sydney. That was Denise's private business.

*****

Sydney used Denise's ID to get into the locked parking lot adjacent to the school. He shrugged his shoulders as he walked up the steps and rang the buzzer. *Bad news won't stay under wraps forever.*

When they were settled in Denise's office, John explained the situation.

Sydney sprang out of his chair. "There you have it. It's over. It's done. Why am I not surprised?"

He sank back into his chair, cupped his chin in his hand, and raised his eyebrows. "I should have listened to you in the first place, Denise."

He turned to cock his eye at John. "I guess you win anyway. You get your school."

John sighed. "You might want to change your mind about your offer to subsidize my school, too—"

"No. No, I'm a man of my word, John. You should know that by now. I haven't changed my mind about anything since this project began." *He'll probably do that football thing.* Sydney shuddered. *Accept that which you cannot change.* He filled his glass with water from the pitcher on Denise's credenza.

"Sit down, Syd. Sit down, and listen to me."

Chapter Sixteen

Sydney sat down and faced John, whose forehead was shiny with perspiration.

"It's not just the kids who messed up, Syd. I didn't exactly play by the rules, either. I meddled." He had a sheepish look on his face as he explained the whole encounter with the police and Dennis Worchowski.

"People really don't change all that much, do they, John? You bullied the boy into it, didn't you?" Sydney spoke through clenched teeth.

John sprang to his feet like a firefighter who'd just heard the alarm. "You think I'm still a bully?" He waved his finger in Sydney's face.

Sydney scowled up at him. "You think I'm still a pushover?"

"Sit down, John." Denise made a time-out sign. John obediently took his seat.

Denise addressed her comments to John, but Syd felt the weight of her stare on his own face. "You didn't tell Syd about the assignment, John—the assignment you gave the kids when you met with them and gave them absolution from their sins."

"I did not!" John was on his feet again. "I did not give them absolution!"

Sydney was so amused by the *gotcha* grin on Denise's face that he didn't quite catch the bit about an assignment until John spoke again.

"How'd you know about the assignment, Denise? I didn't tell anyone about that—only the kids." He frowned at her. "Are you a meddler, too?"

Sydney was surprised that Denise had let herself get caught off-guard. Her voice sounded a little shaky as she responded to John's accusation. "I don't think so…"

The vulnerable sound of Denise's voice made Sydney want to rescue her. But before he could think of just how to do that, Denise spoke on her own behalf. "I guess you could say I'm a mother—Melissa told me about the assignment. She's been living with me on the weekends since December. I got my foster care license a week ago."

"Well, what do you know…" John's mouth hung open.

"Now will you sit down?" Sydney made an exaggerated show of stiffening his neck to look up at John. "I've been living with her on weekends, too—her and Melissa, since last weekend."

John sank into his chair. "I guess we're all of us meddlers then, aren't we?"

"I guess. Let's have it then, John." Sydney sighed. "What's this thing about an assignment?"

After John explained the assignment, Sydney leaned back in his chair and put his hands behind his neck. "You've taken it out of my hands then, John. I guess we'll just have to hear them out. Next week is spring break. Let's schedule something for right after that."

Sydney was puzzled, but he had to admit that just maybe John had rescued the project. It was a long shot, but Sydney had other things on his mind when he left Denise's office.

Melissa wasn't due for the weekend until the next evening, and Sydney was joining Denise in Washington Highlands. He could hardly wait to tell her about his next experiment.

Chapter Sixteen

It was an unseasonably balmy April evening. After they'd finished their Chinese carry-out, Sydney and Denise sat on the screened porch overlooking Denise's backyard flower garden. Sydney put his arm around her shoulder as they gently swayed back and forth on the glider. As they kicked back and sipped an after-dinner cognac, they commented about the bulbs that had pocked their fragile heads through the cool earth.

"Ever been to Paris, Denise?"

"I could have gone with Fred. He went to Europe frequently on business trips, but I wouldn't leave the children, and he refused to take them."

"What about after—when they were older?

"By the time the children were grown, Fred had found a new traveling companion. I guess I just poured myself into my teaching."

"You had summers off. You could have gone then."

"Alone? I suppose I could have. I've done just about everything else alone. But I had this dream. I wanted it to be special. Maybe I'm a romantic, after all."

"That's real fine with me, Denise. I like it that way. How about I make it special—would you and Melissa like to join me in Paris for spring break?"

Chapter Seventeen
Spring Break in Paris—An Interlude
April 1997

They sat in first class, in those cushy leather seats with plenty of legroom and a flight attendant all to themselves. Melissa had the window seat with Denise at her side. Sydney was across the aisle.

The flight was smooth and uneventful for seasoned travelers, but Sydney was delighted when he saw Melissa grab Denise's hand and squeeze it hard for take-off. He smiled to himself as Melissa closed her eyes tightly and Denise squeezed back. When they were gliding above the clouds and the ride became more stable, he noticed Melissa taking a tentative look out the window. She was still holding Denise's hand.

He sat back in his seat and reminisced about his first flight. He was ten years old and petrified. They were on their way to Israel—to Jerusalem. Jerusalem had been a concept to him, not something real. It was something he knew was important to his parents—but at age ten, the only thing on his mind was his fear of flying. He slipped back into that pleasant time in his past when he was comforted by reassuring touches and looks from his parents, a time when he had a naïve trust that the parents whose love he never questioned would protect him from harm and pain under all circumstances.

He looked across the aisle and caught Denise looking back at him. They exchanged a smile. *The frown lines in Denise's face have been relaxing over the past few months. She looks younger, softer. Melissa is different too—more animated, but at the same time more relaxed, not so stiff. They're good for each other.*

The plane arrived seven hours later. Sydney might not have consciously considered it, but for him, it was in that airplane flying miles above the earth that the three of them became a family.

*****

In Paris, they had barely dropped off their luggage before they began the tourist routine. Melissa was overwhelmed with the sights, the pace, and the contagious good mood she shared with Sydney and Denise.

They went to the Eiffel Tower and experienced the gardens and the vendors surrounding it. They saw the live sculptures—young men in body suits who moved just slightly out of their view, tweaking their perception of reality—and the crazy hat vendors who had hats to sell from all corners of the Earth. They went to Montmartre, where the street artists enticed them to purchase one-of-a-kind caricatures for a hefty price. They visited Sacre Coeur, Notre Dame, and Saint Severin. They did it all.

Melissa experienced taste sensations she'd never had before. Even bread—especially bread—tasted different in Paris. She and Denise reveled in being pampered by impeccable waiters. Sydney lavished baubles and delicacies of adornment upon them. He laughed heartily and encouraged them to accept the outrageously expensive Parisian designer garments he helped them choose.

When Melissa became uncomfortable about the gifts, she pulled Denise aside on the pretense of finding a women's restroom. Denise assured her that Sydney didn't have strings attached to his giving. "Sydney likes to spend his money," she said, "and he has lots of it. Choose whatever you like. It's OK."

Melissa took Denise at her word, and she let herself go. The two of them were like schoolgirls together, picking first this and then that, laughing and giggling about matching the colors and styles of their choice. Sydney waited patiently as they disappeared into dressing rooms to try on their selections. He made them laugh when they came out of a dressing room and saw him sporting an outrageous woman's hat.

They all chuckled together when they talked about the spectacle Melissa would present when she greeted her classmates in her new Parisian attire. When they got serious about it, they agreed the wild and extravagant things Melissa had chosen would be inappropriate for her to wear to school, back in Wisconsin. Except for that one reference, they didn't mention home. They were here in Paris on holiday. Wisconsin could wait.

When they arrived, laughing and spent after the day's fresh thrill, in their hotel at night, Melissa was sensitive to Denise and Sydney's need to be alone. She excused herself on the pretense of having a good book that demanded her attention.

Reading, however, was the last thing on Melissa's mind. She was discombobulated, disoriented. Alone in her room, she lay on the bed and tried to sort things out. Sydney was beyond her comprehension. He teased her in ways that didn't make her feel all queasy or scared. When he touched her shoulder or her hand, she didn't feel the impulse to run as fast as her legs could carry her—or even to pull away.

She had seen things and done things that were beyond her capacity to even imagine before Denise and Sydney entered her life. This infectious good mood, this playing at being a family in a fantasyland might turn out to be just that—a fantasy, a pause in her otherwise hopeless life. Her fate, at least for the time being, was in the hands of others, and Melissa was unaccustomed to trusting others. *What's going to happen when we leave this utopia and go back, back to…to what?*

*****

In the wee quiet hours, while Melissa was trying to sort things out, Denise and Sydney were sharing their bed like two ordinary parents concerned about their offspring. They discussed whether to take Melissa to the Moulin Rouge and quickly agreed the experience would be too traumatic for her. Moulin Rouge was on hold for another time, when the two of them would return, for that would surely be another kind of experience. Right now they were being parents, parents in Paris.

Sydney reminded Denise that she'd once asked him why he didn't just abandon his crazy idea, his experiment, and take his grandchildren to Paris Disney. Perhaps they'd take Melissa there.

Chapter Eighteen
Show and Tell
May 1997

Show and tell time. The judges were in their chambers. The kids were waiting in the courtroom.

The students chose the dining room, with the feudal oak table and the oversized chairs, for the final verdict. The walls there had absorbed the many thoughts, words, and feelings exchanged during their meetings over the past several months.

The twins were the designated leaders. They purposefully sat themselves across from each other so as to observe every flick of the hair, every almost-imperceptibly raised eyebrow, and every slight change in expression, decipherable only between them. The others had come to trust them, their intuitions, and their ability to talk and explain things clearly, especially when they functioned as a team.

The judges, Sydney, John, and Denise, had quietly taken their places in the three empty chairs at the table. The children had been careful to seat all three in a row on one side of the table. They wanted to make it difficult for the adults to make eye contact with each other and exchange unspoken messages.

The teachers and house parents were allowed to observe, but not to participate, from the back of the room.

Jenna had made seventeen neatly typed copies of a previously agreed-upon document on her computer. The students all had their copies in hand. She passed copies to the teachers and the Sweeneys. Then she faced the judges and used her most commanding voice as she handed their copies to them.

"Let's all take a moment to read this, please." The students held their breath as the heads of their judges bent to read the papers in hand:

Dear Mr. Schuster,

We're sorry if we have disappointed you. Maybe we're not good enough to accomplish what you've asked us to do.

We have come to the conclusion that we are never all going to like each other. We're not going to be best friends or to tell each other our innermost secrets and feelings. We're not going to share the same pleasures or value the same things. We are not going to understand each other on a deep level. We think that's asking too much.

But we are going to be able to get along if we follow a few rules.

These are the rules for getting along with people.
1. Be nice first.
2. Notice when someone is nice and be nice back.
3. Stand up for yourself when someone is nasty to you.
4. Never be nasty first.
5. Be fair. When you're nasty back, remember once is enough.
6. People make mistakes. Be forgiving.
7. Accept an apology and give a second chance.
8. Give an apology when you do something wrong.
9. Don't be jealous when someone has good luck.
10. Live in the present. Don't hold grudges.
11. Seek help from a trusted adult when you're in more trouble than you can handle on your own.
12. Your personal safety is the most important thing!

Respectfully submitted by:
Eduardo "Eddie" Cortez
Maria Guliano
Karter Johnson
Tashina Jones
Mohandas "Moe" Shastri
Sam Smith
Jenna Stein
Rebecca Stein
Melissa Whistler
Dennis "Demon" Worchowski

The judges, the teachers, and the house parents respectfully took a few moments to consider what the students had submitted.

Sydney stood up, cleared his throat, and made a somber speech.

"You broke my rules, and you've made rules of your own. At the same time, you've caught me off-guard. I expected excuses and explanations for what you've done. I expected you to appeal to my generosity and to try to convince me to excuse you for having broken my rules. You haven't done that, and I respect you for that.

"I need some time to look more carefully at what you've submitted. I know you're all anxious, and it will be hard for you to wait, but please understand, I need to be sure. Ms. Hanover, Father John, and I will take an hour or so to discuss what you've presented to us. I would like your teachers and your house parents to be available to us for consultation. We'll reconvene in about an hour. We might have some questions for you at that time."

The housekeeper brought a tray with coffee, tea, and cookies into the parlor of the rectory, where the judges, the teachers, and the house parents had gathered.

Sydney skipped the coffee. He sat on the couch with a contemplative look on his face and said nothing.

Denise poured herself a cup of coffee. "I don't get it. I'd always tried to teach my students about the importance of empathy. These kids just slipped right past it."

"I've counseled kids to try to be friends with each other." John held the paper in his hand and shook his head. "Are they telling us friendship isn't important?"

"They've just skipped past all the feeling stuff and went for the behaviors. What motivates cooperation if it isn't caring about the other guy?" Denise walked to the window and looked out.

As the discussion moved to which students submitted which rules, the teachers were invited in. Wayne Beemers said he didn't have a clue. Jodi Maxstadt was noncommittal about who said what. She was, however, impressed with the critical thinking of the group, albeit somewhat primitively articulated. Denise knew exactly what Melissa had contributed, and John offered some ideas about some of the others.

Finally, Sydney spoke. "I like it."

The others stopped their analyzing and listened as Sydney went on.

"I have one burning question, though: Did they cooperate? Or was there some coercion involved here? Are there some rules that some don't agree with? Did they just let themselves get talked into something they don't really want or really don't think will work?"

Sydney stood up. "I think it's time to call them back to the meeting."

When the whole group reconvened in the dining room, Sydney took the floor.

"As I understand it, each of you has made a valuable contribution to the construction of your list of rules. Is that correct? Everyone had a voice?"

Jenna answered simply, "Yes, Mr. Schuster, that's correct."

"Which part did you contribute, Jenna?"

Jenna stood. "As you know, Becca and I are Jewish. We believe the Torah teaches us to retaliate when we're wronged. An eye for an eye and a tooth for a tooth. Most people don't understand that."

Becca was about to chime in, but Jenna waved her off. "They think it's justification for violence and revenge. We pointed out that its one eye for one eye, not more and not less than was done to us."

"I see." Sydney raised his eyebrows and scanned the group. His eyes settled on Tashina. "How about you, Tashina? What did you contribute?"

"I ain't Jewish, but I agree wit Becca and Jenna here. I think me and Karter might a gone overboard fore we figured out dat once is enough. Me and Karter agrees on dat now. Ain't dat right, Karter?"

"Yeah, that's right." Karter stood up. "There aren't a lot of things we agree on, but I think it's only fair to give back once. Twice or three times can get you in a lot of trouble— sometimes more trouble than you can deal with." He looked at Tashina. "If you value your life, if you expect to survive, you better content yourself with once."

"That's very interesting, Karter." Sydney scanned the room again. "What part did you add, Maria?"

"The being-nice part. I figure that if you're supposed to give back what you get, being nice ought to be part of it." Maria looked proud of herself as she grinned. "It could be a smile for a smile just as easy as an eye for an eye."

Sydney smiled back. Before he had a chance to call on another student, Eddie jumped in. "Yeah. One time, Becca asked my advice. It made me feel real good. Not like we was gonna be friends or anything, but we could talk about something that was bothering us both, like equals and all." He looked at Becca and blushed. "She was nice—first."

"Rule number nine." Sydney called out. "'Don't be jealous.' Where did that come from?"

"Sir." Moe raised his hand. "We, all of us, wondered how it happened that both of the twins were chosen to participate in the program. It did not seem this could have happened by coincidence. I explained to the others that it really didn't make a difference. Their good fortune did not detract from our own."

"Hmm." Sydney turned to look at John first and then at Denise. "I see."

He turned back to the students and cleared his throat. "Where did all this apology and forgiveness come in?"

Moe took the floor again. "It is me who is responsible for everybody's loss. The others, they had every right to punish me for it. Instead, they said we have got a problem here. Let us see if we can solve it."

Karter chimed in, "Sometimes you gotta apologize if you want to save your own skin."

Sydney nodded at Karter and went on. "Melissa, I'm pretty sure I know what you added. How about you, Sam? What did you contribute?"

"To be honest with you, Mr. Schuster, I don't go for all that religion stuff, like God and the Bible and the Torah and all. Whatever." He shrugged. "I thought we were wasting a lot of time trying to agree on which book had the better lessons. I told the others we don't really need these books to tell us how or why we should get along with each other, and it doesn't matter how we got here. We're here, and it's better for all of us if we just live and let live. These are good rules, Mr. Schuster, no matter who said what before we were born."

Sydney nodded. "That leaves you, Dennis—I mean, Demon."

"That's OK, Mr. Schuster. You can call me Dennis. It's my dad's name. Like Melissa, I guess I agree that when you need help, when you got a problem you can't solve by yourself, you should go to a trusted adult. I didn't exactly go to Father John here, but he helped me admit I had a problem. You know, face it, do something about it."

Sydney and John exchanged a knowing glance, and Sydney concluded the interview with one last question. He handed each student paper and pencil. "This question is to be answered in silence. There will be no need to put your name on the paper. Here's the question. If you could eliminate only one of the twelve rules, which one would it be and why?"

Karter raised his hand and asked, "Do you want us to write the question first, before we write the answer?" He looked at Mr. Beemers with a big, wide grin on his face, and Mr. Beemers grinned back in good-natured fun.

"No, Karter." Sydney signaled his reassurance with a smile. "That won't be necessary,"

The answers were collected in a bowl, and Sydney opened them one by one. He carefully unfolded and read each answer out loud, neatly put the papers down in a stack and reached for another. All the answers were the same.

Chapter Eighteen

There were no rules that could be eliminated. They were all needed.

Sydney placed the last paper on top of the pile. With noticeably wet eyes and a pleasantly painful lump in his throat, he made one simple statement.

"All have contributed, so all shall have prizes."

Epilogue
August 2001

If you were to visit St. Joan's School in Menomonee Falls, one of the first things you'd notice is the large plaque prominently displayed in the entrance. A smaller one adorns the wall of each classroom.

The Twelve Commandments of Proper Conduct

1. Be nice first.
2. Notice when someone is nice and be nice back.
3. Stand up for yourself when someone is nasty to you.
4. Never be nasty first.
5. Be fair. When you're nasty back, remember once is enough.
6. People make mistakes. Be forgiving.
7. Accept an apology and give a second chance.
8. Give an apology when you do something wrong.
9. Don't be jealous when someone has good luck.
10. Live in the present. Don't hold grudges.
11. Seek help from a trusted adult when you're in more trouble than you can handle on your own.
12. Your personal safety is the most important thing!

Respectfully submitted by:

Eduardo "Eddie" Cortez
Karter Johnson
Maria Guliano
Tashina Jones
Mohandas "Moe" Shastri
Sam Smith
Jenna Stein
Rebecca Stein
Melissa Whistler
Dennis "Demon" Worchowski

Handcrafted copies of the plaque were presented to the students of the experimental school, Father John Murphy, Sydney Schuster, Denise Hanover, Wayne Beemers, Jodi Maxstadt, and the Sweeneys, courtesy of Dennis (Demon) Worchowski, carpenter.

*****

Sydney and Denise were married on a warm October afternoon at Denise's house. They wrote their own vows. Father John Murphy respectfully bypassed the sacraments and the Bible readings as he tied the legal knot. It was a small affair. They had a gala reception in Chicago after the honeymoon. Denise convinced Syd to invite Simon, Sarah, and the boys to the reception.

They didn't make a prenuptial contract. They agreed that people weren't married unless they mingled their money. If people didn't trust each other enough to hang in through the rough spots and be fair about money matters, they probably shouldn't get married in the first place, Sydney and Denise reasoned.

Denise was ripe to retire and grateful for the opportunity. She and Sydney immediately took full advantage of being remarkably compatible traveling companions. In the four years since their marriage, they have journeyed to Africa, Europe, Hawaii, Australia, New Zealand, Asia, and the Bahamas.

Sydney took up sailing again, and Denise has proven to be a great first mate. Home base, however, is still the Chicago penthouse.

Melissa was overjoyed when she accepted Denise and Sydney's offer to adopt her. Sydney was grateful for the opportunity to have another shot at parenting, and Melissa has blossomed into a delightful young woman. Sydney wanted her to pursue a career in anthropology, but he wasn't surprised when she showed an interest in psychology instead.

Melissa's attempts to get her mother into drug treatment—so far—have failed. Her mother told her straight out, "I don't want to quit, and you can't make me." Her mother did agree, however, when Melissa found a rescue for her younger sisters. They're living in a foster home with a nice, middle-aged couple whose own children are grown and married. Last Melissa heard, her mother was pregnant again, and her older brother had taken off to who knows where.

Chicago is home to Melissa now. She's chosen to attend college there and continues to live at home, in the penthouse, until she sorts out some of the links between her past and her future.

She's still cautious about being alone in the company of men, except for Sydney—and Kevin. She likes talking with Kevin. She also likes traveling with her parents, and does so whenever her school schedule permits. But Kevin's good company when her parents are traveling by themselves. Sydney and Denise are pleased that he's there to keep a protective eye on their daughter.

*****

Eddie Cortez got himself out of the restaurant business. He used the interest from his prize money to finance his stay at a college prep boarding school.

Eddie's father is still naïve about how HIV is transmitted. He cautiously restricts himself to maintaining the premises and keeping his hands off anything to do with food preparation. Sophie is fast becoming an astute businesswoman and an excellent connoisseur of haut Mexican cuisine. She hopes to make the restaurant a successful enterprise in the future.

Eddie comes home for an occasional weekend, and he doesn't even mind busing tables once in a while. It keeps him close to his sister.

Eddie will be on a pre-med track next year. He intends to research HIV and AIDS after he gets his degree.

*****

When Karter Johnson graduated from the boarding school he attended with Eddie, he didn't choose a cheap college in order to use the money saved on "more interesting things." He's chosen to go to a prestigious university and major in political science instead.

Karter treats his mother with a little more respect since she's agreed to let Kathryn go—although he can't hold back an ironic grimace when he thinks of where she is.

The convent next to the school at St. Joan's was turned into a group home for adults with special needs. When the appropriate time came, Kathryn left home like any other normal young adult. She lives at St. Joan's. During the day, you'll find Kathryn working in a day care center. She changes diapers and feeds and rocks the infants. In her spare time, Kathryn likes to go bowling with her friends, and she takes her birth control pills religiously every morning.

*****

Tashina Jones seriously considered becoming a Jew and going to the Jewish Day High School along with Becca and Jenna. After she set her head to figure "dat" one out, she decided in favor of a secular school. She told the twins, "Us Jones women don't need no old man sittin up there in the sky tellin us what to do, pushing our buttons, and doin our biddin. We takes care a ourselves. We jus goes by the 'once is enough' rules."

True to form, she's kept herself drug-free and unattached. She doesn't carry a knife these days, and she's changed her way of talking. She's already finished her first year of college. Right now, she's working on a practical degree in business, but she's fascinated with geology, biology, and astronomy. She's lost touch with Maria, but she and the twins have stayed in contact with each other. Karter Johnson calls her occasionally.

*****

Becca and Jenna Stein seriously considered going to the boarding school with Tashina, but they wouldn't go without their brother, Ralph. They settled for the Jewish

Day School and agreed to live at home so their money would stretch to include Ralph's tuition there.

The twins and Ralph adhere to "The Twelve Commandments of Proper Conduct" in their dealings with Erica, and tensions in the house have subsided.

The twins did not graduate ahead of time. They were content to be with their old friends in their old school. And the "sticky, stinky half-kids" turned out to be kind of lovable, after all.

Jenna is considering law. Becca thinks she might like to pursue a career in acting. She's been talking to Tashina about lessons in how to talk like an urban street kid for a part she has in a new version of "West Side Story" being put on by a community theater group.

Ruth is still in the nursing home. She seems comfortable and content. Ralph and the twins don't visit her as often as they think they should.

*****

Maria still prefers to be nice, but she's learned to limit the amount of nice she's willing to give. She wants something back, something in return for her kindness. Although she doesn't like it, she's become quite capable of being a little nasty when taken advantage of.

Maria's little boy, Joseph, just had his fourth birthday. Maria used the interest on the prize money to finance day care for him. With the support of her parents and the day care, Maria has been able to graduate from her local high school along with her class. She's considering junior college—and Rodney Marshfield. Rodney is two years older than Maria, and a sophomore at the University of Wisconsin-Milwaukee, and he's nuts about little Joey.

*****

Moe Shastri also got permission to share his portion of the prize. "He is not my twin, Mr. Schuster," he said, "but we are very close." He and Jahan attended a private high school, and they live at home with their parents. Jahan has one more year to go before he graduates, and he plans to join Moe at the university. They've taken to helping their mother run the household. Moe loves to cook, and he's earned his kitchen privileges. He cooks "American style."

At first, Moe stayed in contact with Maria and little Joey, but when Rodney Marshfield arrived on the scene, Moe was relieved. He likes Rodney, and he's happy for Maria. He's not so sure about the Indian bride, though. He still likes "American-style" girls. She's only six years old. A lot can happen between now and when she's ready for a husband.

*****

Sam was disappointed that his high school didn't have a football team. But his parents chose the school, and he acquiesced—especially since Moe would be his classmate. He took up golf instead. He's a natural athlete, and golf turned out to be his forte. Tiger Woods is his idol. Moe Shastri is his coach and his cheerleader. The two of them have chosen a college on the West Coast, where the golf season is long.

Sam's learned how to deal with his little brother, Marty. He just goes by the rules of conduct. They work.

*****

The Worchowski family moved to Menomonee Falls and joined St. Joan's Parish. Demon didn't end up giving the prize money back to Sydney Schuster after all—at least not yet.

At his parent's insistence, the interest on the money is being used to engage a professional tutor. Since his reading skills have improved some, Demon is able to sit still without fidgeting. He will graduate, on his own merit, albeit a year later than his buddies.

Demon is the star quarterback on his school team and loving every minute of it. He still intends to join his father's business when the time comes, but he has another year of high school to go, and he's keeping his options open.

*****

John Murphy was the most significantly influenced by his experience at the Schuster/Murphy Experimental School. As had been promised, he did get the capital to reopen the school for the children of St. Joan's. He did not, however, create the all-boys high school of his dreams. Instead, St. Joan's is an elementary school with a heavy emphasis on cooperative teaching methods. John didn't just listen to the children; he heeded their advice.

That's not all that changed at St. Joan's. John's sermons shifted from a dogmatic emphasis and an individual relationship with God toward encouraging social justice and cooperative relationships between people—shifted from one of prayer to one of action. He's developed a talent and a skill for storytelling. On the pulpit, he passionately breathes life into the scriptures, using them as metaphors for everyday situations. His liturgies are enthusiastic and dynamic. He gets people involved—involved with social reform and involved with each other.

John Murphy's reputation as an activist grew quickly. His parishioners, many of whom are disillusioned by the status quo preaching offered in their more conservative neighborhood parishes, travel as far as thirty miles from the inner city and from wealthy suburbs to join St. Joan's. They are of different ages, races, and cultures. They fill the church to capacity each Sunday.

Small groups gather in the rectory several times during the week to plan and participate in liturgies, to organize adult education classes, to discuss social issues, and to make plans for action.

John is an unconventional priest. He walks a thin line when it comes to the church's official stand on birth control, divorce, homosexuality, and rules for the distribution of the sacraments. His bishop would prefer him to be more conventional and less vocal. His parishioners love him.

Online Discussion Guide
For Book Club Members!

Check out our online discussion guide, available for free at the author's Web site. Surf over to
http://www.LaCourt-M.com/
and help your reading group enjoy *The Prize* even more!

Acknowledgments

I am fortunate to count atheists, Christians, and Jews (alphabetical order to indicate equality) among my family members, friends, and colleagues. I am deeply grateful to them for our many open discussions. I hope I have represented their views without bias.

My three daughters, Jodi Maxstadt, Jana Guggenheim, and Joy Magestro, have contributed unwavering patience, understanding, and encouragement. Jodi was particularly understanding of my need to talk and talk and talk. She's a wonderful listener and a conscientious and honest critic. I especially appreciate Jodi's continued engagement during the rewriting process. Jana pointed out some important inconsistencies and omissions in the plot, as well as some idiosyncrasies of Jewish culture and religion. Joy has been one of my most loyal supporters in this as well as my other writing endeavors.

I thank Patty Barrett, who is also my business partner, and Mike Mattlach for their generous help and support. They traveled with me through the first writing of each chapter, offering suggestions and encouragement along the way. Mike was particularly helpful in providing valuable insights into what it's like to be a twin.

My dear friends Eve and Elliot Lipchik have enthusiastically encouraged me. Their critique of the book was thorough and specific. They said it needed a prologue. It did, and I added it.

I sincerely thank Emily Heath, with whom I have had many stimulating debates about the value of football, and Cregg Kuri, with whom I have had many ongoing discussions about reciprocity.

I told a good story and submitted it to American Book Publishing Group. My editor, Abigail Mieko Vargus, has been indispensable in helping me to write a good novel. Thank you, Abigail. I will miss you when this journey has been completed.

There is a very special person without whose support and understanding I would not have written this book, or anything else. My husband, Bob Stone, is a man of immense patience, wisdom, and tolerance. He is my harshest critic and my staunchest cheerleader. I hope I am the same for him.

About the Author

Marilyn La Court was the stay-at-home mother of five children before embarking on her academic education and professional career. In 1971, she entered college, where she had the delightful experience of attending some classes with two of her daughters. She graduated summa cum laude with a degree in secondary education. In 1976, she earned her master's degree in communication.

Marilyn is a state-certified marriage and family therapist in private practice and is the director of Communication Programs, LLC, in the Milwaukee, Wisconsin, area. She writes a biweekly column for CNI, a community newspaper with 300,000 subscribers.

Currently Marilyn lives in Brookfield, Wisconsin, with her husband. She likes to swim, cook, read, watch movies, and entertain family and friends.